CW01095925

Life is a Movie

By Samman Akbarzada

KINGSLEY
PUBLISHERS

First published in South Africa by Kingsley Publishers, 2021
Copyright © Samman Akbarzada, 2021

The right of Samman Akbarzada to be identified as author of
this work has been asserted.

Kingsley Publishers
Pretoria, South Africa
www.kingsleypublishers.com

A catalogue copy of this book will be available from the
National Library of South Africa
Paperback ISBN: 978-0-620-94129-7
eBook ISBN: 978-0-620-94130-3

This book is a work of fiction. Names, characters, places, and
incidents are either a product of the authors imagination or
are used fictitiously. Any resemblance to actual people living
or dead, events or locales is entirely coincidental.

Dedication

A day doesn't go by without me wondering how lucky and blessed I've been to have a loving family, supporting friends, amazing proponents and I can't help but wonder, how can I be deserving of such precious people. I often think about where I would be without them, and I can't even imagine. But there is this one special person, my mother. She was the reason I wrote my first poem when I was a six-year-old girl, blissfully watching her writing. This book wouldn't even exist without her. She allowed me to enter her wondrous mind where I saw crystal clear what the people in the Graveyard of the Empires had gone through. Besides being an excellent storyteller, she has been my best friend and the sweetest mother I could ever ask for. So, here's to you Mummy, thank you for making this possible and for making me who I am today.

Prologue

The Hero is Born

After seeing the bride for the first time on their wedding day, he breathed, satisfied, and pleasantly eased since she looked like he was told; she resembled Rekha flawlessly. The timid bride (as she was expected to act like) hadn't gazed up yet, from the moment she sat in the chair adorned with rose petals and shimmering shawls. The groom was seated next to his wife, whom he would call Rukhsaar. He asked her more than once if she needed anything. Perhaps he couldn't think of what else to say to break the ice.

It was a festive night when everyone was on their best behaviour, danced, and ate. However, they weren't satisfied since the *khala's* (auntie's) *Kabuli Palaw* didn't have adequate lean meat. And they gossiped about how once the bride shamelessly laughed but quickly held back. They said a few words rooted in their grudges and played their required roles. And just like that, the wedding celebration was over, and everyone left to go back to their homes...

~

Colour drained from their faces after a young nurse brought a family the news, saying, "It's a girl," while gazing down in guilt.

Perhaps the reason she said it in her desperate, tamed tone, as if she said, "It's a tragedy," was because they knew their society. They had created the rules; there was no justice in it for a girl. Deep down, they felt guilty for another victim born. Each one of them was the villain, continuing their evil legacy.

Content cheers echoed all over the hospital the moment another family in the waiting room were informed, "It's a boy." The news earned the young nurse a cash bonus.

"Masih, that's what I'll name my son," said the man clothed in his khaki battledress.

Chapter 1

"Wow.... look, father! The blonde girl pulled out clothes for the two boys from her tiny bag. How do they make it like that? Oh, she is waving her magic stick again!"

Their faces were pressed against the cold-hard window as they gawked at their neighbour's television, both of their homes in the same yard. The neighbour's painted walls and stylish curtains looked much more appealing. The drapes were pushed aside; as a result, their LCD screen could be seen in the corner of their living room, over the polished table.

"Can you read what's written on the screen at the corner?" asked the father, squinting and snuggling in the stitched blanket to deal with the unbearable cold.

"Yes! H-a-r-r-y P-o-t-t-e-r..." the young boy voiced out each letter.

"Is that how English is read?"

"No, but that's actually how I can for now."

"Focus on your studies, Masih, don't end up like me."

"I'm incredibly good at English *padar* (father) it's all our *besawaad* (illiterate) teacher's fault! All my classmates who know more have taken special courses, but you know what? I'm even better than them. Don't you worry, once I get into grade five after winter vacations, it will be the second year of me studying English, and I'll get full marks! I actually did this year, too, in case you forgot."

"Yes, yes, of course only God can compete with this rapid tongue of yours..."

Masih stayed facing the window. "*Padar*, what if life is a movie? And we're being recorded, like right now...am I the *bache film?"* (hero)

"Our life is like a movie *bachem* (son) but, like those tragic ones...however, if you worked hard, not gave up and fought against the bad guys that will come in your life, then you'll become the hero, you'll have to earn it."

"Just like you fight with the bad guys! I wish I could see you in those moments."

"There's nothing much to see but guns and dead bodies lying around the war zones. Anyway, I have good news for you, but promise to keep it between us, okay?"

"What is it?" Masih squealed.

"Next time, I'll come home with a TV."

"Our own?" Masih cried.

"Our own." His father smiled.

"Masih! Masih! Come and help me carry the wood inside, you lazy boy."

"Now go, you little *Shaytaan* (Satan). Your uncle is calling you."

Masih stood up swiftly and dashed out. Unwillingly, he stopped at the doorway and glanced back at his father, who was glaring at him. Both half-smiled at each other. Masih gulped and said, *"Shab bakhair"* (good night).

His father responded, saying the same words, and added,

"Aren't you sleeping in this room tonight?"

"No, Bibi jan isn't feeling well, so I'm sleeping in their room tonight in case she needs me. She said to leave you alone since I don't let you and mother sleep by babbling all the time."

His father smirked, shaking his head.

In bed, Masih had his face fixed at the other side, staring at the light coming from beneath the door, daydreaming about the TV he was promised.

Would it be those thin ones? Like the neighbours have. Will it be loud?

The perfect spot would be beside the door of their own room, so he could have it all to himself...

I want this thing so much that I'm constantly daydreaming about it. It's a bittersweet experience, ugh!

Chapter 2

But You Promised

His eyes opened, then narrowed, glancing at the moulded ceiling. Outside, the morning birds chirped delicately.

Masih sat yawning. He blew his stuffed-up nose into a tissue. Being deserted in his uncle and grandmother's room made him uncomfortable.

His grandmother wasn't in the room, but he heard her muttering coming through from his parent's room across. Masih opened the door, and she resumed her full-throated cursing.

Masih stepped into the room. She was tucked in the corner like a scared toddler, clenching her walking stick close to her chest. "What is it, Bibi *jan*?" he asked.

"What else? Your dramatic mother got sick again. Fainting right after my son left and now because of her, my other son is also freezing in the cold..."

"Where did father go?"

"Oh, you know very well where. Where else can he possibly go?"

"But he had just arrived yesterday!"

"He got a call on his cursed phone. They ordered him to come back urgently since their army base has been attacked again. Curse this government."

Masih trotted outside.

"Where are you going!" she called out.

His cold feet dangled over the four steps of stairs, swinging back and forth. His eyes were fixed on the rusted gate.

It never gets better, none of our problems, it never gets better, my tragic story never changed...

A frigid tingling on his neck chased away his pessimistic self-talk; Masih neglected it once but felt the tingling again. He glared up and shut his eyes when something went directly past his gaze. Masih stood up and covered his eye with his hand. His heart raced in dismay.

His breath quickened, yet he found the courage to uncover his eye. He let out a sigh of relief when he could see past the walls of the garden.

Masih's frown veered into a beaming smile as he was engulfed by the soft diamonds falling from the sky. He opened his palm, and one snowflake landed precisely on it. He stared at it awestricken. Its velocity increased, and so did his joyous prancing under the pouring sky.

The gate opened, giving rise to the obnoxious squeaking sound as always, and his mother stepped in ahead of her brother-in-law.

Her eyebrows raised, and she screamed at Masih to go inside. While reeling towards him, she daunted him. Her thin wrist had a hefty peripheral venous catheter attached to it.

Masih entered the house, his mother and uncle followed.

"Oh, Rukhsaar! Did you pour water after him or not woman?" Bibi *jan* asked as soon as Rukhsaar entered the home.

Rukhsaar refused to answer Bibi *jan*. She sprawled on the cushions, catching her short breaths.

"Mother, when is he coming back?" Masih asked, massaging her legs.

"He will be back soon." she twisted the wedding ring on her finger, then left to the kitchen.

"Be back for what? I assume he's intending this. It's on purpose since whenever he does come, he can't even talk to his old grieving mother because lady Rukhsaar doesn't even let him breathe outside that room! Curse you all..." His grandmother's muttering continued, and Masih's mother kept destroying the kitchen by hurdling the dishes inside the door less cupboard.

Masih, however, couldn't listen to them. The music was blaring on the neighbour's TV. The actress was performing Bharatanatyam on *"Manwa Lage"* song.

Masih was in awe over her breath-taking moves, the way she would circle, move her arms gracefully, the way she looked at her left shoulder and back at the camera. She had his undivided attention until Bibi *jan* interrupted,

"Oh, *bacha* (boy). Hey, I'm talking to you! Go and tell your crazy mother if I come and see my dishes broken, I'll send her back to where she came from!"

Little did Bibi *jan* know how good Masih was at pretending. He kept ogling the neighbour's TV as if he didn't hear a word. She lost her mind and wished death upon him. *If God ever listened to Bibi jan, he would first accept her prayers, not her curses she screams all the time.* Masih thought.

Rukhsaar left for the neighbour's home.

~

"Mother, when is he coming back?" Another day, the same question.

"He will be back soon enough," said Rukhsaar throwing a worn-out slipper inside the wood heater. She covered her mouth with her scarf. The dusky smoke besieging her aura made her cough uncontrollably.

"When will the war be over, Mother? Why can't it stop? You said it ended years ago... If there's no war, Father doesn't have to go away." Another night of Masih's endless musing after watching the news reporter informing about the recent clash in a rural province.

"These forty years of war, Masih, has been a traumatic cycle which never seems to end, there are consequences which never seem to fade away...nothing changed much, we just got used to it." Rukhsaar huffed, lying beside him. "Now sleep." She turned to her other side. The pillow clasped her with covert tears.

~

"Is this how one cooks potatoes? Is this your plot now to kill me, with piles of salt?" Masih's Bibi *jan* screamed at the top of her lungs, staring at Rukhsaar.

They all were gathered in a circle around the holed plastic sheet on which they served food. The torchlight on the shelf lit the room since the power was cut off. It usually took up to ten hours for it to come back in winter.

"But it's not even salty," Masih muttered.

"Masih!" his mother called upon him and added, "Don't talk back to the elders! How many times do I have to remind you of this?"

"But—"

"Shut up!" his uncle screamed, making Masih and his Bibi *jan* twitch.

Masih abandoned his food as he went to the dark and hushed room. He lay underneath the same window they spied on the neighbour's TV. It was his niche to hit the sack, more like his sanctuary from everything and everyone. The moon kept playing hide and seek behind the massive hazes.

If father was here, he would've had my back. Oh my Allah, please bring him back soon, please.

In the chilly evening of a random day, the neighbours turned up the volume, listening to an Indian song playing,

"'Jimmy, Jimmy, Jimmy...'"

Rukhsaar simpered and shook her head timidly. Masih imagined she recalled a distant memory. There was something in this smile. Maybe it was the crinkles in the corner of her eyes, maybe the way the corner of her chapped lips lifted extra elegantly. Whatever it was, it was a complete smile.

"Just when she heard about the Americans, she wanted

to move here. She wants to see the Americans! She enjoys the *kafirs* (none-believers) company... *AstaghfurAllah, AstaghfurAllah...*" Bibi jan was 'praying,' twisting the brown beads Masih's father had bought for her zikr, but she liked multitasking.

What can she possibly be thinking about? Is she remembering someone? Masih thought, gaping at the expressions of his mother, which were foreign to him.

"You see how she's smiling? Shamelessly! She was smiling just like this when this song was playing on her wedding day. I caught her chanting this name. I'm telling you, Masih, your mother, is a—"

Masih stood up and walked outside. He overheard his mother, "Oh, Jimmy!" as she grinned.

Who the hell is Jimmy?

~

It was time for Masih to get lost in his favourite land, dreamland. He sat on his blue sheet, neatly spread on the floor by his mother.

"What did they say?" Rukhsaar hissed, looking at her brother-in-law who was sitting next to Bibi *jan*.

"I did call the commander at Ghazni, but he said the soldiers have been sent to numerous provinces due to an utterly important mission..."

"Did they tell his location? Did they say where he's off to?"

"No, I gave his name and details, but..."

"Do call again tomorrow, please I—" Rukhsaar pleaded breathlessly

Bibi *jan* cut her off. "If you love him so much, then give Razaaq the money to buy the phone credit card. My boy borrowed a hundred Afghanis from me today to make the call. We're not millionaires, you idiot. God knows what wrong I had done that he destined such a pathetic daughter-in-law to be in my life."

Rukhsaar was already inside the six-foot kitchen, washing the dishes in a plastic basin. She turned on the faucet but shut it when not even a single drop of water poured down.

~

"Mother, when is he coming back?"

"Soon."

"But it's been three months!" Masih whined.

"Bibi *jan*, please tell my uncle to call their base. Father always made sure to come back in *Nowruz*, but he isn't here now."

"They said he is no longer there." She gazed at the snow.

"What does that supposed to mean?" Masih asked.

"Ask your mother since she stepped into our house everything got ruined, I said...I warned my son to not listen to this satanic woman, we were so happy in the rural area, but she wanted to live in Kabul! Look at your face, you ugly creature. From which angle do you think you look like a city girl! She's been a bad omen, of course, same as her unfortunate mother with her three disabled children..."

"Don't say another word about my mother. I respect and love her the same way I'm trying to love you. I don't like hearing poor about you nor about my mother!" Rukhsaar howled.

"Oh, so you're talking back to me? God, I wish I died but not seen this day!" she screamed until her voice was worn out.

"What is it, mother? What happened?" her son rushed inside the room, still wearing his muddy shoes.

"This woman is going to kill me!" Bibi *jan* rubbed her fretting forehead. "She cursed me! She abused me! Now that she has seen how alone I am without my sons, she saw it as an opportunity to kill me with her words! Thank God you came, Razaaq, please don't go!" She started crying hysterically.

"What have you done!" Razaaq yelled.

"She's lying!" Masih cried.

11

His uncle brutally slapped him and Masih's head hit the window's marble shelf.

"My son!" Rukhsaar screamed and pulled back Masih. His forehead started bleeding.

"What have you done!" Rukhsaar cried.

"Shut up, or I'll make your face bleed worse. You're a woman, so behave like one!"

"No," she said the forbidden word.

Through his blurry vision, Masih swung his weak arms to prevent the muddy boots from striking his mother's face and the pole which his uncle brought later to hit her on her head, back, and neck as she was bent and crying for help. No one responded to her, not even the neighbours sneaking looks from behind the curtains, not even the flock of men who passed by her cries crossing to their house. Not even Bibi *jan*, who was smirking, then left to the other room. As always, no one heard, no one saw because no one cared.

Chapter 3

A Thousand Hands Reaching for Bleeding Scarfs

The warmth of her son gave life to her dying body. He had his bumpy head against her back. Rukhsaar breathed after feeling his chest rising and falling with rapid puffs.

"Masih," she whispered.

"Mmm..." Masih deliberately held back his tears. He wanted to cry from the discomfort, for he started to feel the unbearable pain he was granted by his uncle.

Rukhsaar sat after failing to do so three times.

She grinned, glancing at him. The smile was stiff, forced, ugly, unlike her usual smile, a sign for Masih she wanted to cry in pain as well.

"Does it hurt, your head?"

"No." Masih smiled, the smile the same as hers.

"If father were here, this wouldn't have happened. He wouldn't have let that happen. Mother, when is he coming back?"

She frowned as she straightened her back and at last said, "He isn't."

"Where are you going?" Masih inquired.

"To get my sewing machine."

"Are we?",

"Yes," she said, opening the zip of the pillow and pulling out clothes from it. She took a scarf, spread it wide open on the ground, threw the clothes in, and tied the four corners together.

"Come," she said, raising the machine from the ground. Her legs trembled as she stumbled, carrying it.

"Mother, should I help you with carrying the machine?"

"No, you carry the clothes."

Masih was sure something had gone wrong since he could barely see the middle parts of things, everything else trimmed and shadowed. The voices inside his head were syncing with his disorganized heartbeats.

Rukhsaar whirled around to have a last look while holding the gate's freezing handle; two figures stood near the window.

"Let her go, son. We successfully got rid of a filthy burden. We needed a spare room for my new daughter-in-law. You know, your fiancée would love this news."

Rukhsaar stepped out into the dark, and so did her ten-year-old son, Masih, following behind her, each not sure how they were stepping, where they were headed to until Masih finally asked, and she replied, "Just keep walking."

"Mother, there are dangerous street dogs along the way, starving."

"If we survived that creature...we can these too, and don't worry, animals are kinder."

He would secretly stick slightly closer to his mother after the leaves would rustle in the chilly zephyr or when the starving dogs howled. Meanwhile, he babbled some brave words. "You don't have to worry about anything, Mother, you have a grown-up son. I'll take care of you..." He kept talking, but Rukhsaar was lost in thought.

The streets were narrow, pitch black, hushed, smelled of latrines, and the walls enclosing them were tall, almost suffocating them. Yet, his mother kept strolling along with her, who wouldn't keep quiet a second. Perhaps his voice comforted both. To his constant chatter, in response, Rukhsaar continued humming or nodding.

Most of the time, they couldn't see what lay above or beneath their feet. Now and then, Masih would look up at the sky in hopes of stargazing, but he had only seen one or two since the air was contaminated by the smoke coming up the metal pipes pointed at the streets. Rukhsaar urged him to only look straightforward, or he might end up falling inside a cavern.

The grapevines scantily running down from the muddy walls of a house caught his mother's eyes, and she half-smiled, shaking her head as if a memory had crossed her thoughts.

Chapter 4

Forfeited

"Rukhsaar! Rukhsaar! My girl, you are collecting dried grapes, right?"

"Yes, Mother!" the eleven-year-old Rukhsaar yelled in response as she quickly placed back a white kitten inside a large carton of sunflower oil with Russian writings. She glared at the cat inside.

"My poor Mary *jan...*" She pulled away a large scarf covering the kitten's tiny stomach and a bowl of milk. She carefully placed the bowl inside the carton. The timid kitten looked at it and sipped deliberately.

"You stay here, oh, and don't meow, meow, please." Mary gazed up at her and continued drinking her milk.

Rukhsaar threw the green scarf over the carton. Now it appeared like the grass and the surrounding willows.

"Hurry up a little. Your aunt Wajiba and I are waiting to prepare them to make raisins!" a voice came through indoors.

"Yes, Mother!" she yelled, running into the fallen grapes over the green sheets covering the ground.

Rukhsaar fetched a basket near the pool of their mini garden and swiftly proceeded to collect the dried grapes when her mother appeared behind her, hands on her hips.

"What did I tell you, young lady! What have you been doing all this time?"

Rukhsaar slowly splashed her face with water and whirled around, saying, "Oh, Mother, there were not so many, so I shook the branches for it all to fall; that took all my time." She straightened her back and wiped the 'sweat from her face.'

"And people say I should be happy for my daughter is now my helping hand but look at her! Learn a little from your cousin's. You see your aunt Wajiba here? Her daughters are cooking *bolani* for dinner; learn from them a little." She snatched the basket from Rukhsaar, shook her head, and started collecting the grapes.

"Psst... Psst!" someone from the neighbour's house hissed behind their shared wall that separated their homes.

Rukhsaar took a step towards the wall while her mother kept daunting as she was bent down and doing the job Rukhsaar was supposed to do.

"What is it?" Rukhsaar hissed back.

"What did you do again?" a voice like hers asked.

"Jamila, I've done something..."

"What have you done!"

"Something really bad..."

"You broke another of your mother's antique dishes collection!?" she gasped.

"No, stupid!" Rukhsaar squealed.

"Rukhsaar!"

"Yes!" Rukhsaar jumped to her feet.

Her mother swerved around. "What are you doing there?"

"No... I mean, nothing," Rukhsaar said, shaking her head.

"Take this basket indoors, be quick."

Rukhsaar rushed to the house, carrying the basket. She felt cold and clammy when she saw Wajiba raising the futons and letting them plunge. But before Wajiba opened the cabinet, Rukhsaar cleared her throat and stepped inside the room. Her heart raced. So must've Wajiba's since she sat down swiftly, taking deep breaths.

"Mother said to bring these to you."

"Yes, yes, put it down and go back, help your mother."

"She actually told me to stay and talk with you. You might

feel lonely sitting alone in here..."

"What? No, no, I'm delighted... Ahem, thrilled, you might want to leave now. Look, your mother definitely needs a little help, chop, chop!"

"No! I mean, how can I leave without bringing you tea, my dear aunt? It's not like I have a dozen. You're my one and only."

"Oh, please!" Wajiba said, straightening her dress and turning scarlet.

Rukhsaar smiled, looking at her aunt while pouring green tea, then she left the room.

"Rukhsaar!" her mother yelled.

"I'm right behind you."

"Oh, okay, Bring me the—"

"The... what?"

"Did you hear that?" her mother said, gaping at the end of the yard near the trees.

"Hear what?"

The sound of an object moving inside something was noticeable now.

"Aha! That, again. I think it's coming from near the trees," her mother said, taking a step towards it.

"No!" Rukhsaar cried, and added after getting scared of her mother's frown, "Why don't you..."

The gate opened, and a man carrying his office bag entered the garden.

"Oh, Mother, look! Father has come from work. Salaam *padar*!"

"Something is clearly wrong with this girl... or is she frankly thrilled to see him?"

"What are you mumbling to yourself, Sonya?" Fardin said, beaming warmly at his wife.

"Oh, nothing. Ha, did you hear that?" Sonya exclaimed.

"Hear what?"

"Sh..."

"It's coming from the end. Wait, I'll just have a look," Fardin said, taking a step forward.

Rukhsaar clenched her numbing legs, her heart moved up to her throat. She gulped.

"Wait!"

Chapter 5

What will people say?

"Wait!"

Rukhsaar shivered as the yellow headlights ran towards her and the sound of the engine becoming louder. She leapt backwards in hopes of surviving the disaster.

"Be careful, Mother, you nearly got hit!" Masih cried, grabbing the ends of her robe, but swiftly left it as she moved on.

They were across a deserted highway, lonelier than them. Rukhsaar set the sewing machine on the ground and took a break to breathe. Since they stopped, only one car passed by. Both jumped to their feet after being traumatised by the deafening sound.

"Was it a suicide bomber?" Masih panted.

A man standing on his balcony screamed, and some people fired their guns, aiming at the sky from their rooftops.

"What is going on!" Masih was scared. His eyes widened at the fireworks sparkling in white, red, and green, displayed in front of them. "Mother, look!"

"We forgot, it's *Nowruz*..." She sighed.

They stood in silence and watched it all.

"Happy new year, Mother."

"Happy new year."

They were now somewhere in the narrow streets of *Bibi Mahroo*, patiently standing behind the locked door.

"Baba must be asleep," Masih whispered, yet Rukhsaar

kept knocking on the wooden door with its rounded, metallic handle.

"Who is it!?" a croaky voice growled.

"It's me, father, Rukhsaar." The door was opened in a split second.

"Rukhsaar! What are you doing here in the middle of the night?"

"Salaam, Baba *jan!*" Masih beamed but gazed down, not getting it back.

"Do you want me to go back?" Rukhsaar took a step back.

"No, no, I mean come inside, consider it's your own home."

"It's supposed to be," she murmured.

They went inside the substantial garden. The two-storey house was lit at the very end of the lawn. A silhouette of a woman in her gown sneaked behind the curtains.

Beside the gate was a petite door. The old man, however, led them inside the room next to the gate. Before they sat on the worn-out futon, Rukhsaar looked at another small door inside the room, asking, "They are in there?"

"Yes, they just slept."

"Mother, I want to sleep." Masih yawned.

The man went inside the little, shadowed room that was shut and brought a yellow blanket sprinkled with holes here and there.

Rukhsaar lay down the two yellow pillows at the corner. Masih crashed the moment his head touched the uncomfortable pad.

"You two sleep. We will talk tomorrow."

Rukhsaar nodded, and she too fell asleep in a matter of seconds despite her swollen and throbbing feet. She was afraid to straighten her back for fear of the dreadful ache, her head felt as if it was bursting, and her exhausted and beaten body continued needling from head to toe.

The next morning, one loaf of bread was cut into four parts, spread at the corners of the red plastic sheet, along with a few spoons of sugar in a jar and two cups, one missing its handle, the other chipped.

Rukhsaar was the first one to stretch out her hand. She reached for the golden kettle and poured tea, then grabbed a piece of the hard bread, which crunched as they took a bite. She put it directly in front of Masih then her father poured tea in the other cup.

No one had spoken a word since they awakened, and the little door remained locked.

Masih finished the rotten bread and lukewarm tea, even though he liked it hot, he was without a doubt heartily appreciative for it.

Rukhsaar looked at him. "Go and have a look at their yard, you like flowers, and they have plenty of them."

Masih nodded and was gone.

"So, tell me, what did you do?"

"What did I do? Farhad hasn't come back since he left to the battlefield three months ago. They treated me like an animal, I adjusted. I took it all but, Father, till when? How much more can I? Doesn't my bones ache? Doesn't my heart wreck? Am I not a human? It's not just about me now...his uncle Razaaq raised his hand on Masih. You did see the open wound on his forehead, which I covered with burned cotton earlier?"

"These things happen between—"

"I'm not going back!" Rukhsaar snapped as she cut his sentence.

For five minutes straight, no one said another word. Her father broke the intense moment. "I believe you understand my condition. I'm an old man who's a doormat. I have three...I have others to take care of. You know well yourself, living as a woman alone is not appropriate, my child, you must think about our dignity. What will people say? There is only one way, I'll talk with Masih's uncle Razaaq, perhaps he will accept you as his second wife after he got married? Or maybe marry both of you in one day, that would be economical too..."

22

Chapter 6

Eyesores

Rukhsaar held her son's hand firmly while carrying the bundle of clothes on top of her head and the sewing machine in her arms, strolling in the bazaars of *Khair khana*.

"We're free!" Masih beamed, prancing.

"We're homeless," she responded.

"We can live on the streets for some time until I finish my school and find a job, even though today is a holiday because of *Nowruz*, but we used to catch up, me and my classmates, I should've been there." Masih peeked at the wristwatch of a man passing by. "*Kaka* (uncle), what's the time?" he asked the man.

"Seven in the morning."

"See, Mother *jan*, it's still time. Do you think I'll make it there in an hour?"

"You are not going to school."

"When will I go to school, Mother?"

Rukhsaar stopped and bent down. "Have you gone mad? My child, I also wanted my son to be educated, but tell me, how am I going to pay the rents all on my own? We can't be homeless. They'll kidnap and sell our organs!"

"I won't ask this question again," Masih murmured.

"And there is one more thing. I don't want you to ask me about—"

"I know about whom, I won't." Masih cut off his mother before she could say whom.

Her eyes welled up, but she seemed to fight back the tears.

He's not dead, he's not dead, and I hate them all for thinking this way, he's on a long mission, saving lives, killing the bad guys somewhere in Afghanistan, and he'll be back and bring a TV, and we'll live so happily. I'll go to school. I hope Mother also gets it and stops being so dramatic. If he was dead, we would've known that day. Masih drew in a long breath.

The streets were adorned with artificial sparkling flowers hanging loosely from the plastic ribbons tied on the streetlights.

Cheerful families stepped out from their homes all dressed up, ladies wore their best gowns, appeared radiant in various colours, kids flew kites and carried toy guns and joyously leapt around, and men were about to start their shiny cars. Rukhsaar and Masih, however, gawked at them and received stares filled with pity in return. Some fearfully pulled their children closer to encourage the two homeless burdens of the country to leave that area.

"Mother, I'm hungry..."

"Keep walking, we'll reach there soon, they will surely have something to eat for us, but don't you dare ask them yourself. I'll take care of that."

Masih nodded, eagerly looking forward to it.

"Hazara!" screamed a man, arguing with another furious man standing in front of him.

Masih stopped.

"Mother, what's wrong with being a Hazara?"

"Ask the man who said it."

"*Kaka*, what's wrong with this guy being Hazara?"

The man raised his bushy eyebrows and took a step towards Masih. Rukhsaar pulled Masih towards her and nudged Masih until they were far enough from the man.

"Are you crazy?" she gasped.

"But you said so!"

"I didn't know you were stupid enough to ask him!"

"If you don't tell me, I'll ask that man again." Masih halted.

"Nothing! Nothing is wrong with being a Hazara, a Pashtun, a Tajik a whatever! We are taught to love our tribe, our province rather than our nation. We are taught who to hate, not who to love. That's what's wrong!"

~

This time, the door she knocked on opened quickly. First, they entered the six-storey apartment. They feared ruining the elevator or getting trapped since neither had used one before. They preferred the marble stairs and stopped at floor number three.

A woman about Rukhsaar's age opened the door, but she appeared more appealing by her groomed impression, her hair twisted in a messy bun and her face covered in unblended foundation. "Rukhsaar!" she beamed but refused to lean closer to kiss and hug, a form of traditional pleasantry in Afghanistan. "Come in."

"I assume you are off to somewhere, Jamila? I'm sorry, I think we should go..." Rukhsaar took a step back.

"What? No, no, I won't let you go like that, you've come after such a long time! Yes, I am going somewhere, but there is plenty of time till I finish my make-up. I might as well do yours too; he won't even recognize you when you go back home."

His mother didn't laugh. Tears shimmered in Rukhsaar's eyes. Jamila gazed at Masih, and he had the same expression. Jamila must've sensed something was terribly wrong.

A few ladies were in the guest room having a loud conversation. One told an adult joke for which Masih's cheeks felt as if on fire. Rukhsaar's friend rushed them into another room and closed the door.

"What is it, my sister? Why do you look so sad? What's worrying you?" Jamila asked.

The strong woman who Masih idolized for taking all his Bibi *jan's* daunting curses and mutterings, his father's

25

commands, complaints, and sometimes sombre attitude, and his uncle's abuse had now had enough. His mother didn't seem to care about her brave reputation being besmirched, nor cared about what the ladies would say about her behind her back. She covered her face with her dry hands as she sobbed hysterically.

Her friend paled and closed the window. She sprinted to her and wrapped Rukhsaar in her arms. "Stop, it's alright, it's going to be fine." She held Rukhsaar firmly.

Masih was experiencing every child's nightmare, his mother's tears.

Rukhsaar explained what had happened after Jamila bought them *nowruzi* cookies, which were large circle-shaped cookies, exceptionally delicious. Beside them were rot, another circle-shaped sweet, its texture between a cream-less cake and a hard cookie.

Masih rejoiced to have all the cookies and *rot*, and the strong, steamy hot black tea precisely tasted the way he liked. His mother's friend begged for him to have more, making him feel like the happiest little boy.

Jamila pointed at her own forehead while looking at Rukhsaar. She, in response, tilted her head towards Masih while gazing at Jamila.

"His uncle..." she shrieked. After that, Jamila shook her head, showing sympathy. She left the room and came back carrying clothes. "My in-laws and I are off to somewhere. I would love to take you two with us, but...you know how they are; I can't change a person's way of treating people, I can't make them kind..."

"I can understand, dear. You don't have to explain." Rukhsaar smiled warmly.

"Take a bath, both of you, and wear these clean clothes. I swear I just pulled it out from my son's and my dresser. Make yourself at home until I come back, then we will figure out a way."

"Alright, Masih?" She flipped her bangs, and Masih found

her relatively charismatic.

Masih nodded, his arms folded while wearing an innocent smile, appearing as polite as possible.

They locked the door after they were sure the guests had left and stepped out of the room.

For the first hour, Rukhsaar was unstoppable. She collected all the cups and dirty dishes from the rooms and washed them. Next, she vacuumed the room, careful not to break the machine since it was her first time using one. When she switched it on for the first time, Rukhsaar jumped in terror and left the room. After her heart's pace returned to normal, and it stopped throbbing while taking a deep breath,

she turned the vacuum on. Its deafening sound was torturous for both. She held no other choice since there was no sign of a traditional broom. Masih covered his ears, singing, "*Shakoko jan.*"

The first one to come out fresh and glossy from the shower was Masih wearing a black shirt with the teenage mutant ninja turtles printed on it. Its edges were frayed. The blue jeans had a hole near the hem.

She didn't just pull out blindly as she would do for her son, auntie was pretending to be too kind like I was being too polite, nothings true if it's too good, there's just something so wrong about something being so right...but at least she's treating us better than others, like humans...

While Rukhsaar was in the shower, Masih had the opportunity to wander around the modern house without being held back.

He opened the lounge door three times but couldn't make himself turn on the massive LCD TV. Masih went to another room which had a TV like their neighbours' — ex neighbours — hanging on the wall, so he did what they did, and the TV turned on.

In his every attempt to change the channel, he would get a chill running down his spine. He noted at least three cartoon channels for which he was so grateful.

Living in this house, which appeared a mansion to him, merely him and his mother, was a dream. He secretly did wish for the owners to never make it back to this house but later felt despicable for his evil wish.

He delightfully watched three episodes of Tom and Jerry back-to-back. It was time for some advertisement which he loathed, even on the neighbour's TV. Back then, he would wander around their tiny room, his eyes still fixed on the window, the window he used to cry hysterically and beg his mother to not cover with plastic to prevent the cold because that way it was impossible to see through. It would be simply a blurry vision of colours.

Even though Rukhsaar constantly would get mocked for not covering them with plastic. She would take it all as a loyal soldier for the sake of her son's happiness. She had done it once but had to rip the covering off since Masih would stand in the cold outside, refusing to step back in the house.

During the never-ending, boring, and repetitive ads... Masih felt the urge to mute the TV and abruptly heard a piece of soft music. The sound was familiar. He stepped outside of the room. The Happy Birthday melody came through a room his mother warned him not to go into. It was the only room left unseen by him.

Why doesn't she want me to go in? What can be there? What are they hiding from me? Is... this house haunted?

His endless questions and theories flew around his eccentric mind. He did bitterly wait for one whole minute, and that was as far as he could take.

The music stopped. Masih carefully took steps towards the room. Other sounds came from the kitchen as his mother cooked: the sound of boiling oil after something was poured over it was one of the sounds, he loved the most since it was a sign that something was cooking.

He was surprised he was by himself. He realised he was

nervous, anxious, and sweating profusely, yet dying to know what was inside.

Come on, Masih, you're the hero! You shouldn't be afraid. The bad guys should be.

His quivering small hands firmly covered the door handle, yearning to open once he finally got the courage. Masih inhaled and opened it quickly.

His eyeballs expanded, hundreds of toys were spread all around the floor, all kinds of them, the kinds he had seen on the cartoons on the neighbour's TV.

A blue bed in the shape of a car lay at the corner, and the whole room gleamed in blue, Masih's favourite colour.

The picture of a young boy, the same age as Masih, was hung on the wall, the boy was wrapped in the kind lady's arms, and a man having an intense gaze, wearing a half-smile.

The kid seems like an ungrateful brat to me... the mother is cool. All mothers are cool. The father...mmm, there's something fishy about him, too serious, I assume... at least this boy has a father who can be mad at him.

The moment he saw the picture, he judged them all. His eyes caught a shiny, black toy car lying overturned near the door. He rushed to it and up righted it.

From the heavy impression and the vibrations of its tiny tires, he recalled it was one of those you pulled back, and it moved forwards automatically. Masih had one of those, his father gifted him on his last birthday. It wasn't this efficient, though. However, he cherished it, then ended up recklessly shattering it into pieces.

He couldn't stop himself. Masih kneeled and strongly pulled the car back on the hard ground, feeling its vibration. The strong whooshing sound was music to his ears, a feeling of power, a sense of nostalgia, an act of aggression, pulling it backwards. When it should've moved forward, the toy car jammed, not rolling an inch.

Masih raised it, and a tire fell over. He threw it away as if it

29

were a headless doll, he feared the most. His heart throbbed out of chronic fear. He gulped, cursing himself, which reminded him of Bibi *jan*.

Perhaps she was right...I'm worthless, I'm ruthless, a bad omen, maybe it's her prayers being accepted.

He closed the door carefully and ran back to the room. His hands were too shaky to clasp the remote again and jump on the other cartoon channels, horrified he might ruin it too. He

sat straight, gawking at the TV, his heart sinking in shame and an ocean of stubborn guilt. His skittish eyes were glued to the screen, yet his soul wandered in his dream room, looking at what he had done.

What would they do to him when they find out?

~

Rukhsaar came into the living room to check on him and saw Masih watching Tom as he was trying to impress the pretty white cat. The cat reminded her of someone...

Chapter 7

White Robberies

"Wait!" Wajiba called.

Fardin whirled around so did Rukhsaar and her mother.

"Salaam brother *jan*. When did you come? And now you're leaving without saying hi?" His sister wore her pink slippers, standing on the doorstep.

"Ha-ha no, no Wajiba *jan*, how can I leave without saying my salaam to my dearest sister?"

"Brother, I was waiting for you. There is something important I need to tell you," Wajiba said, glancing at Rukhsaar going pale.

They all left indoors while Rukhsaar took a deep breath.

"Psst! Psst!"

Rukhsaar dashed towards the stool at the corner of their yard and brought it near the wall. She stood on it, and a beaming face of a girl her age met her gaze from the other side. Her hair was parted in two braids, tied with red ribbons, and her sparkling eyes colossal as the ocean, green as the willows.

"Are you alone, Rukhsaar?" she asked quietly, saying "Rukhsaar" on the tip of her tongue.

"Yes, I'm alone. I think they know what I have done Jamila, what am I going to do!" Rukhsaar cried.

"Is it in a safe place?"

"I don't know...maybe you can have it for me until aunt Wajiba leaves?" Rukhsaar said, leaning to her.

"Me... but I don't have a place to hide it!"

"What kind of best friend are you! You should help me!"

"I told you this isn't a good idea. You shouldn't have stolen from your aunt's..."

The gate slammed, Rukhsaar's heart pounded uncomfortably in her throat. Jamila left and ran inside her home.

Rukhsaar turned, her cousin Reema stood aloof, her left eye started twitching.

Chapter 8

Nobody's Innocent

The sun glinted at its peak before dwelling deep behind the hills. Mullah *sahib* called the adhan, and Rukhsaar began praying in the living room where Masih continued watching a muted TV.

Just when she finished reciting *tasleem*, there was a knock on the door, and both excitedly dashed towards it. Rukhsaar took a deep breath and opened the door wearing a pleasant smile.

Jamila's little boy leapt inside without saying salaam. Next, Jamila and her pretentious husband followed in, his nose stuck in the air.

"Salaam!" Rukhsaar beamed.

The man nodded, averting his gaze. Her friend greeted Rukhsaar with a smile as luminous as hers and replied to her salaam.

Before anyone could say another word or catch a breath, the brat screamed at the top of his lungs, "Ah! Mother, is that my shirt?"

"Suhail!" his mother called on him, twisting her lips.

"That's my shirt! Take it off, you thief!" Suhail boomed and raged at Masih, who stood motionless.

Jamila slapped her son's face. "Where are your manners! Is this how I have raised you?"

The boy tripped, weeping to his room, and slammed the door shut.

It had been less than a minute since they arrived. Masih was accused of stealing, a boy was smacked, the kind lady was apologising, the man was turning purple as they all now stood in an awkward circle near the entrance, the door still wide open.

Rukhsaar gently closed the door.

"Woman! Come inside. I need to talk to you."

Jamila snickered, assured Rukhsaar everything was fine.

"He's had a rough day and is probably related to work."

Rukhsaar and Masih both read him like an open book.

Rukhsaar went to the kitchen and said to Masih to stay in the hallway till they had finished talking in the living room. However, they could hear a rough conversation, which turned into an insulating argument, then into a man screaming, "Tell your friend to move out as quickly as possible. I swear I don't want to see my son get any more hurt because of them once more! Is this a bloody hotel? I believe not! Tell them to leave tomorrow, before I come from work, they should be gone! Or else I'll send you back to your father!"

He left the room and walked straight to his bedroom, not looking at any other soul. Rukhsaar and Masih stood apprehensively shivering at what they heard.

And I thought Bibi jan was mad... Masih mused.

Of course, the splendid day had to be ruined, more than once for Masih, maybe because he enjoyed it the most, and for his mother since she seemed to be hopeful once more. Life shouldn't dare get them used to happiness. Their sorrows were more loyal.

They were hurt horribly. Every word went straight through the heart, the already wounded ones, piled up along the old ones. Perhaps his son was merely an excuse for him to not be kind to them. Maybe for some, it was hard to have decent decorum, yet easy to be miserable.

Jamila stepped out of the room, forcing a smile. "Mmm, the smell is amazing. What did you cook, Rukhsaar *jan*!?"

"*Kabuli palaw*, I hope it came out good."

"Oh, I'm sure it did."

"Ahem...so just because you eat, you know...comfortably. I'll set up another sheet for you, maybe in here, the hallway... what do you say?" Jamila gently rubbed her hands together.

"Oh...yes, yes, no problem, I can understand. I'll help you with the process."

"Great...you give me the plates; I'll take them inside the room."

Rukhsaar nodded.

Masih watched and thought his mother probably understood the unspoken message.

The screeching voices of the man of the house came through the hallway where Rukhsaar and Masih sat cross-legged having supper, ignoring his murmurs, despairing the insolence, catching up with the satisfactory food.

Masih couldn't stop complimenting his mother's astonishing cooking skills as he stuffed his mouth with *Kabuli palaw* and sips of the cold drink which they shared.

Jamila went inside her son's room with a tray full of the splendid food scenting of cardamom and cumin, her voice almost begging her son came through from Suhail's room.

"They are extremely fortunate to have this house, unlike us. An abundant life, right mother?" Masih said.

"I hope so, my child, if one day you made it in life, son,

no matter if I was there with you or not, don't turn into this...like them. Do you understand? Promise me, it's a will of mine."

Masih nodded while analysing the can of his cold drink, figuring out how much more he got left.

He looked up. Rukhsaar half-smiled shaking her head.

After carefully washing the dishes since Jamila paced, her face gone pale, and begged Rukhsaar not to make the slightest sound, for her husband was talking on the phone. He didn't like the clattering but preferred clean dishes, of course.

35

"You thief! You broke my toy car!" Suhail burst out of his room, sounding raucous.

"Your what?" Masih squealed.

"My toy car!" Suhail yelled. Luckily, the door of his father's office was shut or else he probably would've kicked Masih and his mother out right away.

"Why would I break your toy car?" Masih said, frowning and shrugged.

"I don't know!" Suhail whined.

Masih gazed at Jamila, pretending to be innocent. "Just because I'm poor... doesn't mean you can blame me." Masih gazed down.

Jamila stood in awe of him. She pursed her lips, and daunted Suhail, then led him straight to his room for blaming poor Masih. Masih now had watery eyes filled

with phoney tears.

~

Later, Jamila spread a blanket on the floor near the kitchen door and brought two soft pillows for them.

Rukhsaar lay near the kitchen door, and Masih behind her was sound asleep. She glanced at the clock above the kitchen door, ticking, clicking as the seconds passed by. A door burst open and slammed shut.

"I don't know why I have to deal with all the trashes, you microbes, disgusting little pieces of..." He went back inside after using the toilet.

After an hour, the clock showed the time as one in the morning, and Rukhsaar remained sleep deprived. The door opened and softly creaked, which assured Rukhsaar it wasn't Jamila's husband; she veered around.

Jamila placed a finger on her pressed lips and widened her eyes. Rukhsaar slowly removed the blanket from her torso and sat. Jamila gazed at Masih, his body rhythmically moving up and down.

The two friends teared up, but both stopped immediately,

presenting strength, feeling weakened.

"I know someone from my family. They have an extra room for rent, it has a minor kitchen and a toilet. We will go tomorrow and have a look."

"How much is the rent?"

"A thousand Afghani..."

Rukhsaar covered her face with her hands.

"Don't stress too much. I talked with my husband. You are allowed to come over once a week for doing the chores, five hundred Afghani a month, I even begged him to raise, but he then went crazy again."

"You have done so much for me, Jamila, May Allah always fulfil your desires. I'm still not going to make it to a thousand. I'm afraid even begging on the streets won't help me."

"You have your sewing machine. You can do tailoring?"

"This machine was my grandmother's; it is the only thing I own, it was given to me in my *jeziah*... The problem is that I know nothing about tailoring. My mother-in-law didn't even allow me to breathe, let alone playing with this...no matter how much I try to think positive and put my trust in God, I can't, I'm weak, I had enough."

"Rukhsaar! Stop saying this! This is just the beginning of a good new thing. Your son will be in your height just a year later, *Insha'Allah*. This happens, and he will work with you after school and—"

"What school Jamila? How am I going to let him go to his school? I can't even afford a notebook for him."

"Kids do work for themselves nowadays...*esfandi*, or maybe shoe polishing?" Jamila asked, shaking her head,

"No, no, I'm out of my mind."

"Do you have some spare *esfand* seeds?

Rukhsaar looked up at her.

"Rukhsaar...are you...are you sure?"

"What else can I do?"

"It will be good for him to keep himself busy."

"But school?"

"I have to earn at least a thousand more to pay the rent and have at least a piece of bread to eat once a day."

"You sleep now. I think I heard the squeaking of the bed. He must be listening to our conversation. I've caught him doing that," Jamila whispered.

Rukhsaar sighed and put her head on the pillow, forcing herself to sleep.

Chapter 9

Home Sweet Home

Masih sneaked from the kitchen as Jamila's son was getting ready for school. He clenched his brand-new Spiderman backpack, with a blue water bottle inside one of the side pockets.

Suhail combed his hair in front of the spiky-designed hallway mirrors. He swung around and caught Masih peeking at him from behind the kitchen door. Both kept quiet, and Suhail averted his gaze.

Jamila's husband left their bedroom, his wife carrying his work bag, followed him.

The man took the car keys, held his son's hand, and stepped outside the home, not responding to Jamila's "*Khuda hafiz.*"

Jamila closed the door after sending an air kiss to her son.

Rukhsaar came out of the bathroom after making sure Jamila's husband left.

"Let's first have some breakfast, then we will go to my friend's house. She is expecting us for lunch."

Even though Jamila said the house was near, and there was no need to stop a taxi, it had been almost an hour, and Masih felt dehydrated.

"We are close," Jamila said

Masih was panting. He let out a loud burp. Jamila and Rukhsaar were left wheezing; they needed that, an excuse to laugh a little.

His mouth tasted of honey cream he had for breakfast.

Masih faked a couple more burps, but it wasn't funny anymore.

They finally arrived at their destination. The front door reminded Masih of his grandfather's. It was identical to his.

Jamila knocked three times until finally, the voice of a little girl asked from behind the door, "Who is it?"

Jamila replied, "Me!"

The girl opened, still unsure who it was, but you get a response, and you just open. It would be like that sometimes. It was how it worked.

They walked inside, a small, about six meters of plain grass engulfed the left side of the lawn, which had one large fig tree in the centre, and a cobblestoned path led to the doorstep.

The house was cemented, a favourable sign for Masih. He was terrified of the ceiling in their former house when it used to rain heavily. He watched the news about how families died under debris in rural areas.

The door inside was open. Masih inhaled the scent of *kofta* (meatballs) and saw two ladies in the kitchen cooking the meal. Their heads were wrapped with scarves; no one wanted to find hair in their food. Masih crinkled his nose, thankful for their cautiousness. He didn't want to have to pull a hair from his mouth.

After the courtesies, kisses, and hugs, which Masih did not enjoy, his face almost stuck like glue to the cheeks of aunties who had sweated profusely and smelled of burnt onions, they sat over the carpeted, scarlet futons. Before Masih stretched, his hand to have his third sour candy, Rukhsaar gave him one of those stares. Masih held himself back and finished his bitter green tea. He preferred it black. Nonetheless, he was never asked what he would like. They invariably asked the elders, and kids would fancy whatever was chosen.

How unfair is that?

The meatballs were as tasty as their hypnotising aroma, sour, chilly, and yummy.

So, at last, they came at the real deal...

40

"Now, what do you say, Marzia *jan*? Did you talk with the men?" Jamila asked.

After nodding and having a sip of tea, Marzia, the housewife of the house, replied, "I have talked with my husband. He was deeply disheartened after hearing about what happened to your husband, my sister, but so is life..." She inhaled, let out a breath, and continued, "I wish I could bring it more down for you, but as you know, *Taimani* is a nice area to reside in. I don't owe you anything. I swear we have a family who would take it for two thousand..." She took another sip.

"But my husband refused because of their son who had his eyes all over the place, you know what I mean, sister."

"Yes, yes." They would reply each time, then had a sip of the steaming tea.

The room lay across the green grass they had seen in the garden. After they finished their tea, Marzia escorted them to look at the place. They walked inside the twelve-by-six empty room with one miniature door at the end and a tiny, door less kitchen, its sink gradually leaking.

"It's the last renter's fault! All this mess you see." Marzia defended herself from any gossip which was about to come later.

"I see..." Jamila wrinkled her nose then beamed at Rukhsaar. "Now you like it! I love it. It is perfect for you two, mother and son."

Rukhsaar took a deep breath. Jamila clapped.

"Congratulations!"

Rukhsaar forced a smile.

Jamila pulled out a fresh thousand note and gave it to Marzia, "Her first month's rent."

"No, no, I can't accept this sister. You've already done a lot for me." Rukhsaar attempted to give back the money, although Masih guessed that deep down, she felt relieved.

~

Marzia left and returned a few minutes later with a broom and a broken duster.

Jamila went to the store and bought a bottle of bleaching powder.

Rukhaar fought back her tears, musing,

I hate this world a little more, and I fall in love with it every day...

Together Jamila and Rukhsaar cleaned it while Masih played on the lawn with the little girl's orange bicycle. They were taking turns.

Rukhsaar, however, felt the needling and numbness, probably her exhausted body, which would recover after some rest.

The paint on the walls crumbled, yet Rukhsaar didn't mind. Marzia also loaned her a plastic mat to cover the bare floor, two cups, two plates slightly chipped, three spoons, and one tray.

A few hours later, the little girl knocked on their door. She brought for them the leftover *koftas* from lunch, and mother and son enjoyed it.

A vacant room covered with a worn-out plastic sheet, a

moulded kitchen, a tiny bathroom, but it was home, Rukhsaar's and Masih's home. Rukhsaar couldn't stop smiling. She tried to spread the plastic mat until she was satisfied.

She put the sewing machine in the corner and her bundle of clothes on top of it. However, later, she took it back and put it on the floor for Masih to use as a pillow. He did take her promise that she will also share this pillow with him and not sleep on the hard ground, but Mothers would be mothers. She shifted away to leave him more space once he fell asleep.

The sound of the sewing machine woke up Masih. Marzia was kneeling across Rukhsaar as she turned around the handle while mending a piece of cloth.

"There, that's how you turn the handle and use it. Keep practising for today. If I wasn't busy, I'll show you how to brush the sleeves tomorrow," Marzia said as she stood up, steadied herself by the help of the walls, and she left to her home.

"Mother, you didn't know how to use it? But you've had this as long as I can remember."

"Oh, if only your Bibi *jan* let me breathe for a second, maybe I would've known..."

Masih kept quiet.

Masih yawned, stretching his arms. He stood up, and something clicked as it felt on the floor from his pocket. It

was one of the sour candies they were served yesterday, green apple flavoured.

"You stole candy!"

"No, I didn't steal! They brought it all for us. I just took one!"

"That is called stealing!" Rukhsaar roared.

"But they have loads," Masih cried.

Rukhsaar turned her face to look outside through the window. Her smile faded to a memory.

Chapter 10

Mary's Entrance

"How could you steal and from your own aunt! Rukhsaar! Is this how I have raised you?" Rukhsaar's father mocked her as she was being confronted in front of a room full of her cousins, aunt, and her sobbing mother.

"But they have loads!" Rukhsaar cried.

"SO DOES THAT MEAN YOU CAN STEAL FROM THEM?"

"But I just took one." Rukhsaar covered her face to conceal her warm tears streaming down.

"That was a gift from your cousin's fiancé. You should've told me. I would've bought you one!"

"No, it wasn't a gift. She had just given birth at their home. They have six more! They can have that. I'm not giving Mary back!"

A five-second of awkward silence prevailed as everyone tried to process what she said.

"What?" her father scratched his stubble beard.

"I'm not giving Mary back! They weren't even feeding her properly."

Her father glanced at his sister. "What is this about? What are we talking about?" He threw himself on a cushion and rubbed his forehead.

Her aunt Wajiba stood up and approached Rukhsaar.

"Dear Rukhsaar, you're my beloved niece. Your cousin Reema loves you so much. We all make mistakes when we are younger, especially at your age. Please, I beg you to give back her golden bracelet, please!"

"What?" Rukhsaar wiped her tears.

"Her bracelet," Wajiba said, sounding clear.

Their fixed-line telephone started chiming.

"Why are you asking me? I don't know where it is! I've stolen one of your kittens!" She dashed to the garden and heaved Mary from inside the dark carton, her fur white as snow. Rukhsaar kissed her head and dashed back inside.

"Even if you have to take her back..." Rukhsaar sobbed, falling to her knees, lumps of sorrows were stuck in her throat, which prevented her from speaking. She clenched Mary closer to her chest, and her tears fell on Mary's back.

"Take good care of her..." Rukhsaar sounded brittle as she let go of Mary.

Jamila burst through the door and cried, "It's not her fault! Consider me a witness! Please leave my Rukhsaar alone!" Jamila kneeled and whimpered behind Rukhsaar.

"She's lying! I heard her myself talking with this lunatic girl next door about my bracelet. Is she also involved in this? Of course, she is? I swear, uncle Fardin, they have sold it and parted the money between each other. At least tell me to which store did you sell it to, thieves!" her cousin, Reema, who had gone purple, boomed and said it all in one breath. She was panting and then fainted.

The phone rang twice. Wajiba went and answered, the colour drained from her face as she ended the call. She gazed at Rukhsaar's father. "It was...it was my son, they found it underneath the kitchen carpet..."

The room emptied in seconds, and no other word was spoken. Rukhsaar's mother locked the door after them and started cursing them all as she threw her arms around Rukhsaar.

"Please let me have her, please! I promise I'll prevent you from even seeing it as much as I can."

"You can't have her, not in my garden, but my house,"

45

Sonya said, beaming at Rukhsaar.

Rukhsaar's lips curved; she threw her arms around her mother and hugged her firmly.

Chapter 11

Role model

Masih gawked at the crimson cloth, trembling as the sewing machine ran over it. "What are you doing with it, Mother?"

"Sewing sleeves, it's been five days since poor Marzia is teaching me. She's such a good person."

Not that good mother, I've heard the way she speaks behind your back, no one is that good, she is just less bad...

"Mmm," Masih said instead.

Rukhsaar bent her knees then spread them open. She did this repeatedly; her bones clicked.

"Does it hurt?"

"No, I don't know, it feels strange, probably because I haven't gotten...what do they call it...what was that Marzia said is good for bones?"

"Vitamin D," Masih responded, sounding clever.

"Ah, yes, yes that. Let's have a walk outdoors. It's been four days, but don't ask me to buy you anything. I don't have any spare money."

Masih swiftly wore his black jacket ripped from the sleeves, which he didn't mind at all. It was the bazaar that mattered now and how to make his mother buy him a five Afghani popsicle: those orange flavoured ones, sour and chilly.

He searched for his missing pair of socks under the cushion. He pulled it up, and two hundred Afghani notes fell out.

"Ah, you're also a good actor, Mother." He grinned, leaving

it.

The sun had been obscured by gloomy clouds, Masih's favourite weather. A spooky aura enclosed them. Though the one thing that made him feel odd was his mother wearing something distinct, a long blue robe slightly smeared red at the ends. He had previously seen women wear one. However, he preferred the chic black coat on his mother with a brown cotton scarf, which had yellow blooming daffodils printed on it.

"Mother, why are you not wearing your usual bazaar coat?"

Rukhsaar gaped at a young couple passing by them.

"Mother?"

Rukhsaar twitched.

"I... it's better this way. I don't feel like dressing up anymore."

"But why?"

"He's not here. What's the point?"

"But I am."

Rukhsaar sighed and continued ambling. The orange flavoured popsicle stick was delightful to savour its sour and sweet juice. He had been craving it for a long time.

"Allah!" cried Rukhsaar glimpsing at the dark sky after a thunderstorm struck somewhere nearby.

Masih laughed at her.

"Shut up! You're laughing at your mother, mmm? Are you that old now?"

"Relax, Mother, it's just the *Baba ghor ghori* making noises from above the clouds, don't be scared."

Rukhsaar left to find a tool she required for her sewing machine, and Masih said he'd be roaming outside the shop she went in.

The boisterous crowd interrupted Masih's reverie. He ran to the gathered mob.

A boy his age was lying across broken eggs, squashed all

over the ground as the people surrounded him in a circle. His eyes were going white, his torso twisted, his arms stretched backwards, a white liquid ran down his mouth as he grumbled.

"Put a shoe in his mouth!" a man screamed, to which most beckoned.

"No! Are you crazy! Bring me some water!" shouted back a woman in her black suit and silky scarf.

One of the shopkeepers left to his mart and dashed back with a bottle of water, which the lady poured all over the boy. A few minutes later, he sat up, and people thanked God and the kind lady.

Two other young men collected a few eggs that survived and put them back inside the carton the boy sold them from. Three hundred Afghanis were handed to him by a girl. Gradually, people left muttering and gasping, exaggerating, and nagging. One person stayed; his shadow fell across the boy.

Masih gave the fallen boy a helping hand. He grabbed it and stood to his feet.

"Thank you," said the boy.

"Does this happen to you often?" Masih asked.

"As often as I'm in need of it," he murmured.

"What?"

"Oh, come on, you know it," the boy said, gesturing at Masih's apparel.

"I don't sell eggs. But I'll start working soon."

"Then you better get your acting right."

"That was acting?" Masih howled.

The boy smirked said, "When life plays you like that, there's no other way but to play along." The boy left.

"Move on, we better reach home soon!" Rukhsaar yelled, approaching Masih.

The rain started pouring as the heavy vapours lit themselves.

Masih looked up, the cold drops plopped on his skin, the corner of his mouth turned up while he kept his eyes closed.

49

Rukhsaar drenched underneath her *chadari*.

He jumped over the puddles singing, "*Chum, chum, chum,*" and doing the steps the actress was doing in that movie he had seen on the neighbour's TV. He slightly missed that TV and its remarkable movies. Going to Marzia's home wasn't desirable either; she would start asking him about his father and mother's relationship and what was his mother's plan now as if she didn't know already about all that had happened, ceaselessly sceptical she was.

When they got home, and after daunting Masih for his reckless behaviour and making him wash his clothes and himself with plain water, Rukhsaar's temper cooled down a bit. Masih poured her some tea as an apology since he couldn't say sorry nor I love you, even though he wanted her to know he was sorry and he did love her the most, but he only hoped she knew that.

If only she didn't butt head with me. Masih thought.

Rukhsaar's curved eyebrows were deliberately straightening, and so was her sour face getting back to its typical poker face. "I'm still very angry at you and might never take you to the bazaar again if you act like a freed gorilla every time."

"I was just playing."

"Playing!"

"What else can I do? The school was the only place I used to have some fun."

They were silent for a few minutes.

"If things keep going this way, I'll be able to learn to tailor and start working and do house cleaning. I'll be able to pay the rents and find something for us to eat...so if you want to start your school, save your money, enough amount to buy yourself your uniform, notebooks, and pens."

Masih beamed. "Really!"

"Yes, I've asked Jamila for some spare *esfand* seeds, and she said yes. It's not that hard either. You just circle the can and say a few words."

"I'll do anything!"

"Don't say it like that. People know how to use from your vulnerabilities, say, I will if it was what I wanted to do."

Jamila came to the door. "I hope I'm not interrupting?"

"Oh no, no, come in, Jamila *jan*. We were just talking about you."

Jamila took off her sandals and walked inside the room.

"Good thing I can finally come to your house without getting cursed by Bibi *jan*, mental I'm telling you. Anyway, what were you talking about me? Mmm gossiping about *khala* Jamila Masih?" She snuggled in the only pillow inside, which Rukhsaar put behind her.

Masih faked a smile.

"We were talking about him starting school if he could afford his school needs. You remember I asked you about the—"

"Oh yes, yes, I remember. Well, that would be great. I was honestly really worried about his education. He is your only hope, you know, he must be educated. Well, I forgot to bring it for you; borrow some from Marzia, and I'll bring her from the bazaar."

Jamila left after gossiping about her entire in-laws, didn't leave even one. Masih had to close his ears sometimes to not hear her vulgar speech.

Rukhsaar gazed at Masih as they both were stood in the doorway as Jamila left.

"Masih...I... you know that I hate to send you away for this, but I..."

"Mother, you don't have to feel guilty. This is not your fault, at least I'll be starting school. I'll find a job maybe as a trainee in a shop. We'll sort it out, you don't worry, you just smile. I haven't seen it for a while."

Rukhsaar smiled, fighting back the tears, and strolled towards Marzia's house, her head bowed.

Chapter 12

Eesfandi

A young lady wearing a red blazer sauntered down from a polished black Corolla. First, her high heels stepped down, then her torso. She chuckled and resumed chewing her gum with her mouth opened. Another lady hopped down, and they both kissed each other goodbye: the traditional three kisses on the checks.

Masih had been wandering around for half an hour. He knew this was his time to shine and put on an extraordinary act again. He averted his gaze, walked into her, and chanted the hocus-pocus spell, *"Eesfand balaa band chashme heach, chashme khaish."*

At last, he got her attention. She glanced at him, frowning, in disgust almost.

"Auntie, don't you want to scare away the evil eye? Look at your shimmering golden bracelet. God forbid it might have caught the evil eye of your sister-in-law!"

"How do you know she is my sister-in-law?" she squealed and rested a hand on her hip.

"Oh, *khala jan*, I know I might be little, but trust me, the way she looked at you from the corner of her eyes, oof."

"Wait! Go on, take my *nazar*. Can you do palmistry? Oh, I've always had a feeling about her!"

Masih circled her with the burnt tomato paste can, stained black, a trail of smoke heaved from inside, its black seeds cackled, the smoke twisted around her, its pungent smell spread all over the place and made her cough uncontrollably.

"You see how the seeds are jumping, almost out of the can?" Masih raised the can for her to see closely.

"Oh yes, yes."

"It's a sign..."

"Of what?"

"Of a nasty evil eye... mmm, I see, you should be aware."

"Here, read my palm." She stretched out her hand, and her trembling palm was right beneath Masih's jawline.

Masih held her hand.

"Isn't it the right hand which they read?"

"Ahem, that is for the ordinaries."

"Ah, so you mean I'm special?"

"No, I am," Masih replied

The lady raised her brows, leaned forward, dying to know what was going on.

"Mmm...mmm. Oh!" Masih squinted, then opened his eyes wide, his jaw dropped, and he grinned.

"What!"

Masih took in a sharp breath.

"What is it?"

"I assume it's been a time you're longing for something, something authentic, for something to happen."

"Will it?" she blushed.

"Mmm, maybe and maybe not."

"Maybe when? Any date?"

"Oh ma'am, that would be a five hundred Afghani."

"Oh, no, then leave it. I haven't brought that much Afghani with me. There's no place to change either."

"So, what about my money?"

"I merely have a hundred Afghani, would that do? I'm coming again tomorrow as well. Maybe I'll see you again?"

"Sure." Masih gently took the pink and purple coloured paper, balling his fist, and holding his laugh, dying inside.

The first time he earned a hundred. He placed it securely inside his chest pocket and patted it, half smiling.

The lady was gone.

"Good one, Masih," he murmured.

Chapter 13

Falling masks

"So, how is everything going on with the new life?" Jamila asked excitedly. She was propped at the kitchen doorstep watching Rukhsaar do the piled-up dishes.

"Nothing much," Rukhsaar replied coldly.

"Come on now! You're at last a free woman, be a little happy, I mean, get to yourself a little. I have some spare dresses and some cosmetics I no longer use. I'll give them to you today."

"Thank you, but I don't think I'll use them. Give it to someone who might have a little interest in themselves."

"Oh, sister, I'm trying to make you understand it, but you can't seem to! If he's no more, I mean...I'm sorry for that, and we can't bring him back. You're still young and beautiful, don't you think it's about time you should..."

Rukhsaar half-smiled. "You love once, and you marry once. It's enough for me now."

"He was who you married, but we both know he wasn't who you loved...what if maybe someone came to see you".

"Jamila!" her husband boomed.

"Yes!" Jamila yelled, sounding sweet and innocent from the kitchen.

"Tell the housemaid to make some green cardamom tea, besides it put those milk fudge I bought from Herat on my last trip. You bring it to me. I don't want to see that dramatic woman. She might start crying in front of me again, begging for a penny," he roared from the guest's room.

Jamila gazed at Rukhsaar, who was ogling her.

"When have I begged to him?" Rukhsaar hissed.

"No, no you haven't, but you see, when you first told me about what happened, I told him that you were so desperate and that you cried...but listen, that's only because I wanted him to give me some cash for you, that's how I paid your first month's rent."

Rukhsaar sighed. Taking out a square-shaped iron box from the upper cabinet, she drew her fingers over the miniature picture of young ladies in a prosperous village printed on the golden cover, musing.

He has been a good man, a good husband to me, a great father to Masih, perhaps I would never have found someone as good as him, but what hurts me is that...they didn't care at all what would happen to me, what is my word, what I wanted, it didn't matter, not a bit.

There was a knock on the door.

"Jamila!"

"I'll get it," Jamila said as she whisked for the door and opened it.

"Oh, Salaam, Mr Sultan, how are you, brother *jan*?"

"Ha-ha Salaam, Salaam. How are you? How is your boy?" a grating voice roared, which compelled Rukhsaar to clear her own throat that would itch uncomfortably whenever he began to chatter.

"You didn't bring the family?" Jamila asked.

"Oh no, no, they were invited to their grandma's house today, so I dropped my wife and the kids there. Do you have guests?" He jerked his thumb towards the kitchen.

"No, no, it's the house...it's my friend in the kitchen." She lowered her voice. "The one we talked about that night, whose husband was..."

"Oh, I see..." The man clicked in pity; his voice started getting closer.

Jamila whispered something to him, and he let out a giggle.

"Such a tragedy, so young. I personally felt devastated when Jamila told us about you."

The man stood while Rukhsaar turned her back to him, hiding her face, nodding, clenching her fist, and shrinking into an abomination. He sighed, stepping inside the guest's room. Rukhsaar felt relieved, loathing the stares she received.

She put two Chinese teacups overturned on the golden plate, next to it the milk fudge in a sugar bowl and a golden teapot.

Jamila disappeared. Rukhsaar heaved the tray, her hands trembled, her throat turned utterly dry and enclosed with rigid lumps.

She got closer to the obnoxious laughs.

Rukhsaar entered the room, her eyes fixed at the red rug. She put the tray over the glass desk and kneeled to pour tea from the teapot. They had gone hushed after her entrance; the strong smell of cigarettes forced her to hold her breath.

The man guffawed, muttering something. From the corner of her eye, Rukhsaar saw him glance her way.

"I heard about you, Rukhsaar."

Rukhsaar opened her mouth to say something, but he interrupted.

"That's your name, right? Sorry, I cut you off."

"Yes, brother." She put his cup in front of him on the table, not looking up.

"Ahem, I presume you just walked down from the hills? Ha-ha brother! Tell me, am I your brother? Do we have the same parents?"

"No," Rukhsaar replied bluntly, still avoiding eye contact.

"Then don't call me that, you bitch!"

Rukhsaar took a deep breath. Her hands trembled, and she accidentally spilt the other cup, which she almost served to Jamila's husband.

"Bring a cloth and wipe the floor!" Jamila's husband

barked.

Rukhsaar dashed outside. She knocked on the bathroom door, Jamila wasn't there. She went to every room, but she couldn't find her. She knocked on Suhail's door since it was locked.

"Yes!" Suhail called, stuttering.

"Where's your mother?"

"Umm, she's in the bazaar, no in her sister's house."

Rukhsaar pressed her ear against the door. Surely, she heard someone else mumbling. Rukhsaar covered her mouth with her hand and let out a faint sob. "God, help me."

"Bring a cloth, woman, and put it over the mess you made!" Jamila's husband yelled.

"I'll do it later." Rukhsaar tried to sound strong, adhering herself to the wall, but her voice broke off and trembled.

"Do it now!"

Rukhsaar swiftly wiped her tears. She pulled her shoulders back and walked in.

"Sit and do it."

"Isn't the scarf bothering you? Let me help you with it..." The man stretched his arms towards her as she was kneeling on the ground, wiping the rug.

"Enough!" Rukhsaar screamed and abruptly stood up. "Enough!" she cried, stepping back.

The man sat back on the couch, a shocked look on his face.

"You know that I can destroy your already ruined life?" Jamila's husband said, putting his ankle over his knees.

Rukhsaar remained silent, fighting back the tears.

"Do what he wants, or else..."

"I lived my whole life bearing warnings, warnings of how I'll be sent back to my fathers, warnings of my nose being cut off, my tongue burnt, my pictures going viral on national geographic, my body being beaten as if I'm already a corpse owning a bare soul, but it's enough! Now my life isn't that sweet to me, so I listen and scare away from warnings...your warnings don't scare me, I don't care."

Jamila's husband stood to his feet and raged at her, brutally squeezed her cheeks. They were burning in anguish.

"No! Please!" Jamila entered the room and fell to her knees.

"I had told you to stay in the room!" he screamed.

"Please, let her go." Jamila looked up at him, clenching his feet.

Jamila's husband threw her face away and grabbed Rukhsaar's left arm. He led her through the doorway, squeezed her arm, and threw her outside. He slammed the door shut. Rukhsaar fell on the marble stairs of the foyer and wept.

"Want some help?" A gruff stranger stretched his unsteady arm to her, his stinking mouth stuffed with rappee, his eyes red and drowsy.

Just then, Jamila burst through the door and scowled at him. He disappeared.

She offered Rukhsaar a helping hand, but Rukhsaar stood, grabbing onto the wall, her body impassive, her torso staggered, Jamila gripped her halfway through.

"I'll walk with you to your home."

Rukhsaar disregarded her and strolled outside, Jamila followed.

"Just like the past...you're avoiding talking to me... remember you used to do this to me because you knew I couldn't keep my mouth shut for a second? But those fights never lasted more than fifteen minutes. This one won't, too, right?" Jamila asked, then smiled, gazing down.

"We had more meaningful conversations back then, I suppose. We were understanding, we weren't friends nor sisters it was a bond somewhere in between, way rarer yet we lost it, Jamila. Not in the ten-year separation due to the war, not for the thousand arguments we had, not even that one time when you slapped me, but now. I don't know you anymore, my Jamila wouldn't have done this to me, she wouldn't have sold me to anyone.

"It won't ever happen again."

"We both know well, Jamila, it's not the first time you're letting me down. He loved your father more than his brother, but..."

Jamila paused. Rukhsaar kept walking, then turned back to look at her friend. Jamila's eyes welled up. She turned and headed back to her home. Rukhsaar closed her eyes, and tears softly rolled down her skin.

~

Mullah *sahib* called the *Maghreb* adhan. The sky was dimming. Rukhsaar opened the gate, and a dark silhouette dashed into her arms.

"Mother, I've earned so much money from the rich auntie, Mother, you won't believe me!"

"Get off me, let me go inside."

Masih let her go, they stepped inside.

"How much?" she asked.

"Oh, you won't believe me. A hundred Afghani, it's so new, look!"

He lifted the plastic sheet and pulled out the hundred note, displaying it to his mother, beaming.

Rukhsaar's expressions hardened and slightly pushed him away from her. "Is this too much for you? Don't you know we have to pay a thousand Afghani just for the rent?"

"I thought you'd be happy..." Masih lowered the note and stepped aside.

Rukhsaar stared at him straight-faced.

"What?" Masih asked.

"What?" Rukhsaar squealed.

"I mean, be happy..."

"Masih, I can't be happy for a hundred, maybe even not for a million..." She entered the kitchen, a hard naan was wrapped in orange cloth, and cold black tea was in their silvery thermos.

Rukhsaar brought them into the room and settled them in

front of Masih. A barrier was built, a cold distance enclosing the two sitting across each other, a separation from a mother's love, too ragged to bear.

"Why? Why can't you be happy?" Masih shrilled.

"Get used to it, Masih...my son, get yourself a job or something. This is not enough."

"I want you back, Mother, like you used to be."

Chapter 14

Evanescence

"I want her back like she used to be." The young Rukhsaar, in her teenage years, flipped her hair, saying this to the girl striding beside her.

"Yeah...auntie Sonya has changed so much. I guess it's the hormones and stuff. She's so furious all the time."

"Ugh! Baba really should learn how to cook. We had overcooked rice with almost raw potatoes last night, and you know what? Mother loved it!"

"Jamila, can you hold this for a sec..." Rukhsaar handed her the books she was carrying and put her hair in a messy bun with the help of a blue pen she pulled out from her pouch. Then took out a heart-shaped perfume bottle from her purse and sprayed a bit on her floral dress as well as Jamila's frock.

"Mmm, smells like strawberries...our favourite! You got this new?"

"Oh yeah, Baba bought me yesterday...it's fine, I guess." Rukhsaar took back her books, and both divas swaggered to Rukhsaar's home.

The gate was open, and when they stepped in, the scent of watered roses and fresh mint farmed in their massive yard travelled to each part of their soul. They closed their eyes and inhaled deeply till they were blessed enough.

The two girls dashed indoors, gave their salaam to Fardin, and stopped at the hallway door with blue wind chimes dangling from its curtains. A poster was fastened to the door; it was a collage of distinct species of cats in almost every colour. Rukhsaar opened the door, and a ginger cat moved towards her, abruptly rubbed himself against her feet.

"Oh, Jimmy, how much I missed you! Where is Mary?"

Then came the diva cat swaggering to her and purred.

"Oh, here you are!" Rukhsaar beamed.

Rukhsaar sprayed the room, this time using her bear-shaped perfume bottle from her makeup table, and the cats purred once more.

"This one's peach-scented, Baba bought from Russia in his last trip, my babies like it."

"We'll be having the kitties coming soon, I guess. What do you think, how many?" Rukhsaar said as she drew her fingers over Mary's silky fur.

"Oh, what if *khala* Sonya had hers at the same time as Mary? That would be chaotic!" Jamila nearly screamed, saying this.

Rukhsaar took in a deep breath as she leaned across Mary, who had fallen asleep.

Fardin leaned against her room's door, watching the girls, smiling.

"Baba!" Rukhsaar called, turning to face him.

"Come on, girls, lunch is ready."

"Umm... what about we get the food from..."

"Your aunt Wajiba has brought us *mantoo* . Don't worry, it's not my cooking."

Rukhsaar and Jamila grinned awkwardly, peeping at each other.

"Come now, it's getting cold."

Rukhsaar and Jamila descended the stairs and politely followed Fardin. Rukhsaar felt dreadful, looking at his messy, curly hair, which badly required a cut.

They were back to their garden. The table was adorned with Chinese plates and a large tray filled with *mantoos*. Also, on the varnished table were red roses shimmering in water drops; the sun was somewhat obscured behind the ivory mists. What a fine day.

Rukhsaar and Jamila happily took their seats.

"So how was school today? Learned a few more words in English? Or maybe saw some new people around you didn't see before? Something unusual?" Fardin scratched the nape of his neck, peeked back at the gate, and sat.

"Oh, yeah, it was fine," Jamila said, eating a large spoonful of the mouth-watering dish.

"She'll be alright Baba, I know you're stressing too much about her," Rukhsaar said, looking at his troubled eyes.

"What? Oh no, yes, yes, she'll be alright," he said, averting his gaze.

His spoon clanged as it hit the ground. He fetched it.

"What's wrong, Uncle?" Jamila asked, gazing at him as he shook his legs, staring at his food.

Fardin sighed. His hands trembled. He leaned forward towards them. "I've been... I've been hearing some things."

"What?" they both squealed.

The gate burst open. Sonya entered the house with Reema, once again with their disappointed faces.

Rukhsaar glanced at her mother's outrageous belly, which was concerning everyone. "Mother, but you said it will happen this time. I'm dying to see my baby brothers!" Rukhsaar whined.

Reema and Sonya took their seats. They both were panting.

"Did you see the news?" Sonya asked her husband, breathless.

"What happened?" Rukhsaar shrieked.

Chapter 15

Changing positions

"Mother of Masih! Mother of Masih!" Marzia kept knocking on the door and peeped inside through the blinds.

"Yes, coming!"

"Why doesn't she call you by your name?" Masih hissed while eating his breakfast, which was another loaf of naan with bitter tea.

"Shush!" Rukhsaar gently smacked his head.

"Salaam Marzia *jan*, come in," Rukhsaar said, holding the iron door wide open.

Marzia dashed inside and sat. Rukhsaar heaved the pillow from behind Masih's back and put it behind Marzia's back for comfort.

Masih couldn't believe this, his eyes went wide, but he said nothing. One of the Afghan rules, anything for the guests.

"So, ha-ha, how's everything Rukhsaar *jan*?"

"It's fine...how about you?"

"Oh, really? I was just a little worried since you didn't go to Jamila's today and her friend's home you were starting to work in... I heard a few rumours but—"

"Mariza *jan*, don't worry, there's nothing going on you don't know about. I will find another home to work for, very soon."

"Yes, yes, I'm sure you will since there are only a week and three days left for your rent...I don't want to pressure you just in case you..."

"No, I haven't forgotten, I'll pay you. There's time left."

"Oh sister, I don't want to hide thing's from you..." Marzia threw her hands on her lap.

"What do you mean?"

"I heard what happened to you yesterday in Jamila's house. I swear I didn't tell anyone, but there was someone else who also called me and told me about it. I wonder who is spreading—"

"What are you talking about?" Rukhsaar raised her voice. "Masih, you go outside for a minute," she added, and off he went.

~

"I can understand, sister, perhaps I would have also moved on. There is no way for you to be ashamed. Your husband has—"

"Get out."

"What? This is my house!"

"I'm paying you!"

"Jamila paid me, not you," Marzia murmured, getting up and leaving the house.

~

Marzia stomped to her home, frowning at Masih. He ran towards their part of the yard and saw what he hated the most, his mother's tears.

He swiftly pulled himself back and sat under the window outside so she could cry. She was inhaling hesitantly and sobbing, a squeal then weeping. Masih apathetically gawked at the sludgy wall across him.

An hour passed, Masih hadn't moved. Footsteps drew closer, and he scampered away from the window. Rukhsaar opened the door and shouted his name.

Her face was red, her eyes puffed. Regardless, she forced a smile when Masih walked in. He forbade himself from looking at her. This world kept getting sadder by their broken smiles.

"I'm going outside with my can."

Rukhsaar remained silent. Masih grabbed it from the kitchen's rusted shelf, which was deserted once he took his can.

Young boys in their blue uniform passed across him as he reclined on the edge of the pathway.

I thought I'll be going to school again, how naïve...how silly my thoughts can be, getting back to the normal is only a fantasy now, no more daydreaming.

His can was empty, no more *esfand* seeds remained, and the only cash he had was twenty worn-out Afghanis, safe inside his chest pocket.

Masih ambled in the bustling streets of *Shaar*, a place where they said anything could be found. He was surrounded by men with handcarts, screaming the names of the fruits and vegetables they were selling. Some had loudspeakers attached to them, and the drivers screamed the name of the location they would take the passengers. A woman yelled at her daughter, and the kid screamed at another minor;

everyone was screaming.

Masih stopped across a silver car. Its owner cried out at the top of his lungs, from which Masih understood, he was about to take the passengers to *Torkham*.

He stood there. Could he somehow convince the driver

that someone was waiting for him at the other side, then escape, not knowing where to? Just far away from her tears, from what she had become, run away to a new life, grow up and never come back...

Masih took a step forward.

"Hey, kid!"

Masih turned. A pair of skinny legs were in front of him. He raised his head all the way up to see his face.

The man with his bold moustache gazed down at him. "Are you a working child?"

"Ye...yes." Masih gulped.

"Good, do you want a job?"

He joyfully stared at the wooden box opened in front of him filled with all kinds of shoe polishes, brushes, and black cloths.

"Only four hours a day and that much money, what else could I ask for?"

Masih saw a man from inside a shop across from him watch him. Probably to make sure he didn't run away with that glory box stocked with shoe polishes.

"Did you know? The first thing people notice and see is your shoes! It's a scientific thing, you should watch more movies. Now before you embarrass yourself, come and do yourself a favour."

Masih took the job. Periodically, he changed the pitch of his voice from low to high, making eye contact with strangers, who were the first to look away.

Later in the day, he was enjoying a loaf of bread a kind lady offered him when a black boot appeared on top of the border of the wooden box. Masih raised his gaze, and from the man's black glasses and averted eyes, and a black jeep parked a few steps behind him, Masih knew well what kind of man he was: the wealthy ones. However, when the man took off his sunglasses, Masih now recognised the arrogance this man carried. He was Jamila's husband.

Masih raised his bread for him to hold but instead received a terrifying gaze. He held it between his teeth to enjoy it later.

The man's iPhone rang. He sighed and answered the call, annoyed and without looking who was calling. "What is it, woman? I told you I'm busy...oh sorry, I'm sorry, I thought... Ha-ha, no silly, I thought it was her, you know..."

Masih kept his gaze down and heard the other person on the phone squealing then laughing.

"Mmm, I see...so when are you coming tonight?"

"She still doesn't know about you. I can't."

"What are you waiting for? It's not like we can hide this

forever. I'm also your wife! Why did you marry me if you didn't have the courage?"

Masih paused, the man gazed at him and altered feet, Masih scrubbed, as slowly as he could.

"Listen, my dear, I'm not afraid of her, okay? I'll be coming later."

"Ugh! Okay, come soon. Hey, listen, I love you." she giggled.

"Love you too," the man said in English with an accent, but little did he know if there was any phrase Masih knew in English, it was "I love you," thanks to all the times he heard it in the movies. Then something regarding love

happened after it.

The man shoved his phone inside his pocket. "Enough." He pulled away his foot.

"Twenty Afghani," Masih said.

"You owe me a lot." He smirked and left, acting like a mighty lord as he slammed the door of his car.

Masih cleaned his hands with one of the raven cloths, laughing. Sometimes one can be disappointed to the extent that nothing disappoints anymore, you just laugh.

Chapter 16

Stretched arm, running feet

"Mother! Mother, I found myself a job! After lurking under the sun for hours and asking every man, I saw on my way, thirsty and starving just for you, I..."

"Stop with all this, Masih. I know you."

"Okay, okay." Masih took another bite of the crunchy cucumber his mother bought. "So, this shoe polisher man came to me. I work as his *shagerd* (trainee) for four hours. He will give two hundred a month."

"I see. Why did he give it to you?"

"I don't know."

His mother said nothing.

"But mother! You won't believe what happened today!"

"Oh, Masih, I don't have time for your stories. I have to go and find a labour for myself." Rukhsaar paced out of the kitchen after Masih stepped out of her way.

"It's about *khala* Jamila."

Rukhsaar stopped and turned.

Masih broke the news to his mother.

"I knew he was not a good man. I warned Jamila it's all lies, that he's just after you because you're beautiful; it's all lust. There's no loyal man, he can marry and have the world's most beautiful wife, but when he got the chance and his wife isn't looking, he will wink at a monkey!" Rukhsaar ranted.

"But father was loyal."

Rukhsaar let out a harsh breath in irritation. She left the

house, not saying another word.

Masih beamed and kept munching his fresh and delightful cucumber. He took another from the kitchen and left the house to play with Marzia's timid daughter Sherin. She constantly spoke of the stars with a light in her eyes and how elysian the universe was, she, Masih, and their profound cosmogram. Then she would do her homework, showing books filled with colours and pictures that Masih had never seen in his books since she studied in a private school with fancier books. Of course, Marzia wasn't fond of this friendship. She would shoo him away and call him a germ, though she was nowhere to be found now.

~

After knocking on every door, she came across on her way, being rejected countless times, humiliated by men, women, even children, and abused, not just her, but her entire ancestors, Rukhsaar almost gave up. Panting under the blazing sun, she stopped near a wooden door of a little home to take a break. It must've been a middle-class family, she hoped. Perhaps she could be useful to them in some way or another, so she stopped hesitating and knocked on the door. She knocked once more, and after a minute, she turned, fearful of the setting sun. Just then, the door clicked, and it opened in a slit.

"Who is it?" a trembling voice of a woman asked.

"I'm here for...I'm...do you need any housemaid? I can cook and clean." Rukhsaar's voice quivered the same way as the woman behind the door.

"No, go away. My husband isn't home."

"Please, please, I've been searching for the whole day. There is nothing in the house except for half a kilo of cucumbers I could afford."

Rukhsaar struggled to see the woman's face, it was dark behind the squeaking door, and the sun had now almost set.

The door closed, Rukhsaar held her breath. It made another

71

clicking sound and, to her surprise, burst open. "Come inside."

~

Seven-thirty pm, the sky was darker than the infuriated Marzia. She had come and obnoxiously asked if Rukhsaar had returned. Masih would perpetually make her scream more than once, then he would shout back, "No."

He was scared yet at the same time, glad to see Marzia's curious self about to explode.

At last, the gate opened.

"Where have you been?" Marzia squealed, her hands firmly placed on her hips.

Rukhsaar rolled her eyes and stomped, facing her door.

"I asked you a question! Answer me!"

"I don't remember marrying you," Rukhsaar mumbled.

Marzia pursed her lips.

"I will talk about this to my husband. I'll tell him everything about you!"

Rukhsaar opened the door and slammed it shut while Masih was ogling her.

She handed him the plastic bag she carried. "Fruits."

Masih seized the bag of fruits and started munching. The apples were sweet as honey, and the bananas perfectly ripe, good quality fruit, which meant it was costlier than the fruit they used to buy.

After three large bites, he finally asked, "Where did you go?"

"I found a very decent family who lives at the end of this street, their door was locked when I first got there, but coming back home, I knocked again, and she opened. Her husband is an Arabic teacher, his wife has a *madrasah*, kind family. She sent these fruits for you and invited you to learn in her *madrasah* for free, spare some time for there. I'll go there once a week, five hundred a month."

"So... now we can pay the rents! Five hundred plus five

hundred equals a thousand!"

"What five hundred?"

"*Khala* Jamila's! You're going tomorrow. It's Tuesday."
He was dying to hear a signal, something about if he could go
to school again.

~

Rukhsaar had completely forgotten to tell him about it. *Where
to start from or even what to say. How to say such an evil act
while gazing at those innocent eyes?*

She hummed instead, then said, "Now, don't eat them all
right away. Spare some for your tomorrow."

~

The day began better than yesterday. Masih had five customers.
Until the owner came back, he had polished seven pairs of
shoes.

Masih stood up, stretched his back, and the man sat in
his place, and before he left, he called Masih. Masih swung
around. The man stretched his arm holding two of those purple-
coloured papers, straight and new. "I'm giving you your salary
in advance, don't forget the month, it's May."

Masih took the money and nodded. He left prancing on the
streets. The school kids had been dismissed, and Masih kept
staring at them, slightly envious. Still, he reminded himself
that if things kept going that way, he'd be able to go to school
again.

Exactly when he gave one a strange gaze, he saw a familiar
face. Masih gazed at him from afar as the boy guffawed, his
hands swung over the shoulders of another student rambling
beside him.

The boy paused as he glanced in Masih's direction. Masih
turned his back to him, his heart ached. He was dying for a
reconciliation, but he'd been easily replaced; there was no
point.

Masih crossed the street feeling gutted. He just wanted to go home.

"Please, please help me, just a little I ask from you," a woman cried, hurled at the pathway, begging another woman standing across from her. Masih's heart skipped a beat. He spun around.

"I have a son!"

He stopped in the wrong spot, not because he stood in the middle of the street without traffic lights and no traffic police. It was just him and the cars passing by.

Masih sensed a car coming close to where he stood. He stayed there as his eyes flooded with tears and gazed at the woman who praised the other one for giving her a penny.

The woman in her blue *chadari* which had a crimson stain on its verge. "Masih! Masih! Car! Masih! Masih no! Please!"

He jumped, and the black glassed car passed away, cursing him.

"What are you doing? I thought you went to *khala* Jamila's!"

"They kicked me out..."

"Why?"

"They wanted me to do bad things."

"What do you mean, is this good that you're doing? It must've been better than this!"

"Masih, shut up!"

The crowd paused, glanced at them, and continued on their way.

He and his mother walked back home, both silent. She sobbed discreetly and drew her hand over Masih's hair. He nudged her away and walked faster ahead of her.

Once at home, Masih could no longer keep his mouth shut.

"Did you beg for these too?" Masih muttered while Rukhsaar held the last apple and two bananas from the previous night.

"Tell me, did you? If this was your plan, then I wish we would've died that night. I wish I didn't pull you back when the car was going to hit you that night. I wish he killed us both!"

She swung her hand and slapped him right on his sunken cheekbones. Masih lay his hand on his face, his eyes burned with tears, yet he kept them open.

Rukhsaar lay down and turned her back to him, her elbow propped her face.

You're punishing me, mother, but then tell me, why are you the one suffering?

Chapter 17

Bury a dream

"What is it? What news?" Rukhsaar said, leaning forward.

"The Soviets..." Fardin hissed.

"What? What happened?"

"Not much yet. There are rumours..."

"These are not rumours Fardin, there is war all over the country. We are all going to die." Sonya, his wife, said, sobbing.

"What war? Oh, you're just overreacting. They said it was just a little clash."

Rukhsaar glanced at her polished nails.

"Missiles don't fly around in the city just for a clash," she cried, slamming her hands on the table.

"What missiles? It was just one time." Rukhsaar giggled.

The glass shattered as it fell from the table, songbirds flew away from the trees, the voice then transformed into a whistle, an obnoxious whistle fading, another blasting sound, however, this one seemed to put them in ease.

"It hit."

"Where do you think it was?" Sonya panted; her hand propped over her belly.

"I think...I think it was near Kabul University," Fardin replied.

"God forbid!" she cried.

"You two are not going to your school!" Sonya said, looking at Rukhsaar.

Jamila had already disappeared without them noticing.

"But mother. I have an important exam tomorrow."

"I don't care. You are a young girl. You should know you need more protection than anyone else."

"Baba!"

He left the table and walked indoors, his head hanging down.

Rukhsaar slammed the table and dashed to her room. She locked the door and sprawled out on her bed and took a deep breath. Jimmy and Mary jumped on her bed and placed themselves under her clammy hands.

Rukhsaar covered her face and sobbed.

"I'm sorry...but I promise you, I will not let them steal my dreams. I will finish school, and I will become a veterinarian. I want to be so much more than just a label. I'm not just a girl living to get married. No!"

Chapter 18

Swinging children

Her pillow was drenched with tears. Rukhsaar wiped her face and sat. She lay her hands flat on the floor to aid her to stand up; she couldn't move her legs. Her heart pounded.

"Masih! Masih!"

"What?" he shouted, his back turned to her.

"I can't...I can't sta—" Rukhsaar finally stood after the second attempt. "Nothing, I'm going to the teacher's home. Take these ten Afghani and buy yourself something to eat."

Masih made sure she'd left then got up.

The first thing he did was buy the orange popsicle; afterwards, with the other five Afghani, he bought a biscuit.

A treat for getting beat up!

He laughed, licking his popsicle.

Not so much of a productive day, but it was over. His boss did taunt him, though, and Masih had to develop deaf ears after the man didn't stop howling at him for the polish he wasted.

Finally, he permitted Masih to go home once he poured all his anger over him.

Masih sat quietly on the bench and stared at the kids playing near their school gate while swinging his legs.

He heard footsteps approach, then stopped. The bench moved slightly. Someone sat beside him.

"Your mother doesn't like you very much, does she? All they care about is money, isn't it? She's dying for a penny."

"She's not dying for money. We need money." Masih

glanced at him. He was slim and towering, wore those black suits like Jamila's husband.

"I see...how much?"

"Enough to keep us going." Masih sighed.

"No, no, strive for the best. You have the potential, I see. You can have a lot of money."

"Who are you?"

"Your admirer, young man."

Masih smirked, swinging his head.

"You know? There are people who can help you out."

"Who? Masih stopped shaking his legs.

"Come and see for yourself. If you liked it, we could have a deal."

"Is it hard work? I'll do anything!"

"Ha-ha, not that hard, come and see for yourself." The man stood up, straightened his coat.

"What do you mean?" Masih asked, looking up at him.

"Do you want money or not?" He placed his hand on Masih's shoulder. Even when he let go, the weight of his heavy hand somehow remained on his feeble shoulders.

He got up and followed the man. The man said three times along the way that his office wasn't that far. Masih scratched his head, not believing.

What can I possibly do in an office loaded with computers?

He had seen a computer once in his lifetime, and that was from afar, but the man would know this since it was obvious that Masih was a working child: his dirty, stained hands, ripped leather jacket in summer, oversized, dusty flip-flops, and a weary face spoke for themselves.

The man pulled out a bottle of energy drink from his bag. Masih refused, remembering what his mother always said.

"I don't mean any harm, Masih." He smiled, opening it and took a sip, then handed it to Masih.

Masih took a sip. "How do you know my name?"

"I've been watching you for some time. It's all out of

compassion, you know. I don't offer jobs this easily."

Job...he's giving me a job? I can't believe this!

The streets were getting narrower, yet Masih wasn't afraid anymore. Perhaps it was the caffeine, or maybe the stranger had earned his trust.

The man stopped abruptly in front of a blue gate. He knocked but then pulled the doorknob down, and it opened. His face turned slightly red, and he murmured something to himself.

A two-metres square cemented space then another door, the house was one storey and quite small for an office. "So, is this your office?"

"Yes, yes. We have different branches across the country."

Masih nodded, still hesitant about what to ask.

The man opened the door, and this one wasn't locked as well. "You wait here, I'll call you in."

Masih stood closer to the door in the long hallway. Among three doors, one slid open. It was a pink tiled bathroom; two remaining doors were closed. He pulled down the doorknob of the room closer to the bathroom, but it was locked.

The man knocked on it. He appeared less frustrated now.

Someone opened the door, the person inside held back.

The man walked inside the room and closed the door.

Masih felt something odd under his feet. He raised the mat, which had "Welcome" written on it in cursive, a key lay underneath it, Masih threw the rug back over it.

He tried to eavesdrop on what was going on inside, but he heard nothing as if they were talking in sign language. Masih leaned closer, the door clicked, he pulled himself back, and almost had a stroke.

The man stepped out. "Come in, Masih."

Masih entered. Six red futons were spread all over the room. A large make-up table stood at the corner. He turned to his left, a young, skinny boy wearing a tight burgundy blouse and leggings greeted him.

"Hello, Masih." Something about his tone of voice compelled Masih to step back a little. The boy was chewing gum with his mouth opened and stared at Masih in a way that crawled under Masih's skin.

Masih gazed down. The silver anklet with its heart-shaped rings the boy was wearing impelled Masih to cringe. He averted his gaze and saw a colourful dress loaded with adornments hanging beside the make-up table. Masih's heart thumped. It made sense now. He was dealt with what he knew existed but never believed it might.

His sight blurred; floaters were hopping all over the place. He couldn't concentrate on what the man and the young boy were babbling about, nor why the boy was laughing so much, throwing his hands and flipping his silky oiled hair, which covered his droopy eyes.

"Okay, Masih, you know the drill. Gul will help you with everything. Now make sure this time you've locked the doors!" He gazed strongly at the boy with the burgundy shirt, Gul.

"Ugh, please! Just leave! Go!" Gul pushed him out of the room guffawing and ran back to the makeup table after swinging around and looking at Masih, then winked at him.

"Aren't you too small?" he said, patting the makeup brush all over his cheeks.

Masih opened his mouth but choked on the words.

"What am I even saying? I was five when he first brought me here..."

Masih said nothing and stared at Gul.

"He's my own uncle. Can you believe that?" Gul laughed and turned around.

"I see, you're also from the timid ones. It'll get better." He turned to face the mirror and was now putting on scarlet lipstick. "I'm done now, come it's your turn."

Masih sat on the cushion. His body shivered while he was losing all his senses. Posters were clasped over the walls; one captured a tall boy wearing a flared dress, his face draped with his hair.

"*Kaka jan* said to make you look a little older by make-up or something, he also said to examine your moves and get you ready for our clients, there will be a gathering tonight here.

Masih gagged, covering his mouth.

"What is it?"

"Nothing... I'm... I'm good."

"Good, I'm going to turn on the speaker now. You better show me your best moves. You do know what you've put yourself into, right?" Gul heaved his shirt a little, a gun peeked out from his legging's stitched pocket.

"Mmm, I will, okay." Masih gulped.

"So... you naughty boy!" He set his make-up.

"Low music or...Dambora, which one do you prefer?"

"Dd-ambora."

"You know how to dance? You practised before?"

"*Khai ne* (of course) I'm a natural dancer."

"Oh, I see. Kids these days, huh? So go on now, stand up." Gul turned on the speakers; the man singing had a slurry voice,

Masih couldn't catch up with his words. He could barely listen to the beat he wasn't enjoying.

The boy clapped harshly in a rhythm. Masih froze and shut his eyes. When he opened his eyes, the boy's clapping slowed as his gaze got more suspicious.

Masih endeavoured to recall that dance he had under the rain, over the puddles, as he was jumping and laughing, holding his favourite ice-cream. Would he be able to taste it once more? Or was his life ruined now?

Tears ran down his cheeks as he recalled his mother, her screams, her real smile, the way she would lay her delicate hands over his head to give him her blessings after her prayers. Masih moved his feet left and right, thinking about the actress he had seen in the movie. He jumped.

"Impressive!" Gul laughed aloud.

Masih stopped. "I need to use the bathroom."

"What?" Gul shouted, leaning to him, his hands cupped behind his ear.

"The bathroom!" Masih shouted, his voice broke off.

Gul paused the song with the remote he held.

"I said, I need to go to the bathroom."

"Oh, okay. It's across the room."

Gul sat on the brown chair across from the mirror. "Ugh! My make-up today," he whined.

Masih opened the door slowly, not as if he were in a rush.

"Leave the room's door open!"

His heart throbbed in discomfort. Masih entered the bathroom. He splashed cold water on his face; his shirt was soaking wet. Masih stared at the mirror above the sink. He stared into his fearful eyes and on his trembling lips. Masih sobbed. He bit his lips so as not to make a sound and gulped; silent tears rolled down his cheeks.

Masih stopped crying. He inhaled and looked back. The small window all the way up had thick iron bars. There was no point in struggling to reach it.

He snuck out of the bathroom to the front door. He touched the doorknob. He heard Gul humming to a song. He pulled the handle downwards, extremely cautious not to make a sound. Masih was sweating profusely, his breaths got shorter. He gave the door a slight push. It opened without making a sound.

Masih turned to look; Gul was putting something on his almond-shaped eyes, too absorbed in the task to notice him.

He dashed outside and went next door. He raised the rug and took the key. He entered, and the door clicked, his heart continued racing.

Suddenly, a pair of leaden hands fell over his tiny shoulders and pulled him back to the other room. Gul slapped him three times and grabbed him by his collar.

"You think I'm a fool," Gul said.

Masih felt his face redden by all the brutal slaps, and he began sobbing.

Gul opened the door slightly. A boy carrying a backpack stood still with a slightly crooked spine, his clothes ripped, his face slim, his hair all messed up. The boy took a step forward and stumbled.

Masih pushed Gul away and escaped. He dashed to the gate, which was wide open, and ran for his life, not looking back once.

He bumped into a man who held him by his shoulders. Masih kicked his ankle, not thinking that perhaps the man just wanted to help.

Chapter 19

Rollercoaster

"Masih, are you alright?" Rukhsaar asked.

Masih was ogling the brown sheet.

"Masih!"

Masih twitched. "Yes?"

"What are you thinking about?"

"Nothing..." Masih added, "Are you mad at me?"

"Why?"

"Because what I did today..." Masih gulped.

"What did you do today?"

"Yesterday, about yesterday."

"Oh...no, no. It was my fault. I won't talk like that again." Rukhsaar's eyes flooded with tears. She wanted to hug him and cry, holding him close, and say she loved him so much and that she was sorry for his father, she was sorry he couldn't go to school, but she barely stared at him, imagining...

~

Masih wiped the sheet with a kitchen cloth, folded it, and carried the dirty dishes to the kitchen. He walked to the corner of the room and lay down, then turned his face to the wall. He was still not sure how he was alive. He remembered it like a flash, a dream, a nightmare was the word.

"Mother! Mother!" Masih hissed.

Rukhsaar lay awake. "What is it, Masih!?" she turned.

"I dreamt of Father. I saw him for the first time since he left Kabul! He said he will come back! I told you!"

For the first time, instead of the recurring nightmares of his uncle beating him with his pole, Masih had a dream.

Rukhsaar sighed and sat after struggling to move her torso. She was used to it now, sudden paranoia. We get used to things, doesn't make it any easier, but just imagine if we couldn't.

"Listen, Masih, you're a big boy now, and I'm sure you understand what I want to tell you." she looked through the window. "Your father isn't coming back. Masih, he was a soldier. He has—"

"What?" Masih asked after Rukhsaar's sudden pause.

Rukhsaar looked back; Marzia was standing near the door. "What is the date today?"

Rukhsaar reached her hand, gripped her red scarf lying across her, and wrapped it around her head. She got up and left the house.

~

Rukhsaar and Marzia were having what seemed like a silent conversation as Masih watched their gestures and their lips moving. They were calmer than when they used to talk before.

Rukhsaar nodded, and Marzia shook her head. After a minute, Marzia left.

Rukhsaar entered the room and inhaled.

"What was she saying to you? Was it about..." Masih held back his tongue, remembering his promise. He shouldn't ask about him.

"Yes."

Masih's heart throbbed. He wanted to jump and hug her.

"I said I can only give five hundred Afghani this month. She said this should be the last time but thank God she accepted."

His expressions hardened. Expectations perished from his heart; it knew exactly how to hurt brutally. It was just a dream. Stupid dreams...

"She did warn me it's a loan." Rukhsaar put on her *chadari*.

Masih heaved the edge of the plastic rug and took his three

hundred Afghani. "Here, then it'll be just two hundred. I'll try to do something else too."

Rukhsaar's hand trembled as she took that money. She gazed down and left the house.

~

The next few days went quite well. Rukhsaar had found another home to work at for a thousand a month. Masih continued his polishing, and his pay was raised to two hundred and fifty a month. He told his boss about the man and what happened. His boss said he knew who Masih was talking about and told Masih that the man wouldn't come again.

It was the first of June, Masih's birthday. He woke up to Sherin, Marzia, and Rukhsaar singing, "Happy Birthday." They tried once to say it in English, yet the only one saying it right was Sherin. The rest were saying something like, "You too, to you."

Marzia bought him a small packet of cake, which cost twenty Afghani. Sherin gave him a notebook and a pencil. She also read for him the quote written on the side of the cover, "Quitting might be easy, but regretting is not."

She translated for him, and Masih pretended to be inspired by it profoundly. He sighed and nodded.

The birthday aura lasted for an hour. Afterwards, everyone left back to their houses, and Rukhsaar left for her work. Marzia and Sherin left to their relative's house.

His boss had asked Masih to not come that day since he won't be able to go either. Masih was walking on the lawn, running, kicking the air while adding the whooshing sound effects with his mouth.

The fig trees rustled. One fig fell in front of him, and luckily Masih caught it. Otherwise, it would've splashed all over the ground. It happened quite often.

Masih washed it and had it all in one bite. It tasted sweeter than the cake he had today.

He refused to go home till his mother came or Marzia and her daughter returned.

The sky faded into light blue, and it was time for Rukhsaar to get home before it was dark. Masih unlocked the gate.

She will come now, any minute, so what's the point of keeping it locked?

Just as quick as it got dark, his thoughts did too. He locked the gate. It had been an hour since it was unlocked.

Marzia had turned off the lights in her house before she left for her aunt's. Masih went inside his home when the rustling of the trees creeped him out. He had heard about the sacredness of the fig tree.

He locked the door two times, pulled down the blinds on the window, and sat in the corner while sneaking looks from behind the white blinds to see the gate. A shadow fell over the ground, coming through from underneath the gate.

Masih recognised his mother's feet, though this one was enormous, exactly like his...his heart started thumping.

Is he here for my birthday? Did he wait to surprise me on my birthday? He came back?

Masih ran as fast as he could, and before there was a knock on the gate, Masih pulled it open and opened his arms.

"Father!" he jumped into the man's arms.

The man wearing a white hat gazed at him in fear. It was the most embarrassing moment of Masih's life. Masih took a step back, clenching his fists; his face felt hot.

"Uh...are you Masih? Son of Rukhsaar? I'm the teacher, Noman. Your mother is in the hospital. She fainted while working at our house. I have come to take you to the hospital."

Masih dashed outside of their yard. "Take me to her!"

"Did you lock the house?" The teacher asked.

Marzia and Sherin stepped down from a taxi just then. Marzia rushed towards them. "What is it? What is this man doing in my house, Masih?" she asked.

Noman sighed and gazed down. "I'm the teacher, Noman.

Masih's mother works at our home. She is in the hospital."

"What! What did she do this time?"

"Sister, can you please lower your voice? I'm standing in front of you! *La hawla Walla.*"

"What an indecent person. Come, Sherin, let's go home." She walked inside, crinkling her nose, and lifted her head up to look at the clouds.

Masih and Noman hopped inside the same taxi and were off.

A few minutes later, they arrived at the hospital, and Masih entered his mother's room. Rukhsaar was lying

straight. Her skin was pale, her lips chapped, and her eyes sunken. She smiled her worst one yet. She stared at Masih, who had stopped near the door. Noman left them alone.

"Come and sit, my child. How are you? You must have been afraid alone at home."

"No, mother, I'm fine. What happened? Why are you here? How are you? What happened?" His voice broke off as he fought back the tears yet failed. He sobbed and covered his face.

"Shush...I'm alright, Masih. Just the blood sugar broke down. I didn't eat breakfast. It's my fault. Don't cry..."

"How did it happen?"

"I'm fine now, I don't know yet, I just couldn't move my legs, and I fell. I don't know what happened next, Masih."

Noman knocked on the door.

Masih dashed to him.

Noman was holding a bottle of mango juice.

"Take this and share it with your mother. I am going now. There is a taxi waiting for you. Take her back home."

Noman must've noticed Masih's red eyes.

"Don't worry, son, she will be fine after she rests. I'm sure the doctors will say the same thing too." He turned and slightly raised his voice.

"*Khuda Hafiz*, sister."

Rukhsaar attempted to sit but ceased to function.

"*Khuda Hafiz*, brother. Thank you for everything..." Rukhsaar lay back, pain on her face.

There was a knock on the door, and this time the doctor entered. "Are you still feeling dizzy?" he asked.

"No, no, not at all."

"Headache?"

"Just a little, I'm okay."

"What about the chronic pain?"

"It'll get better."

"I'm afraid this is a critical condition, sister. We must take an x-ray of your back. You show symptoms of an illness. And one more thing, have you been exposed to force on your back? Did you hit it somewhere?"

"Is the machine in this hospital?" His mother refused to answer the doctor's questions.

"Unfortunately, no, you have to take the x-ray outside. It's just across the hospital. It will cost you no more than a thousand."

Rukhsaar gulped. "Yes, I will bring my x-ray to you tomorrow, but I must go home now."

"It would be better if you stayed here. The sooner we get the results, the quicker we would be able to act. This can leave you paralysed for the rest of your life!"

"My husband will take care of me."

Masih swiftly looked at her. She shook her head and pressed her finger against her pale lips and widened her eyes, sending Masih a message to be quiet. The doctor was busy gazing at her file.

"Let's say I am what you said. What will you do? What is the treatment procedure?" Rukhsaar said while putting on her flip-flops.

"For you, the only way will be operating. I'll be giving you a five thousand cut already, so no bargaining."

Rukhsaar nodded and stepped down from the bed. Masih

got hold of her arm, and they carefully walked outside and into the taxi. After the quiet ride, they arrived at their home.

"Operation! They are out of their minds!"

"Don't worry, Mother. I will find that money when I grow up. Until then, you rest."

"Don't you get it? They are lying! I'm alright, son. It's just a little irritation. Marzia has it worst. It's a women's thing. Don't worry, I'm alright, this is Afghanistan, they will do anything for money, trust nobody."

Rukhsaar was lying, and the only pillow they owned lay underneath her back for comfort. Masih poured her some juice, and Rukhsaar said he could have the rest. He gulped the thick mango juice straight from the bottle as Rukhsaar slept.

Masih woke up to a knock on the door, but before he got up to answer it, Rukhsaar already dashed and opened it, she walked fine.

Maybe it was a facade after all, like she said.

Rukhsaar was once more having a serious conversation with Marzia. However, this time, Marzia left soon afterwards, and Rukhsaar kept calling after her.

She came back into the house.

"What was she saying?" Masih asked her.

"It's that time of the month again... she's asking for the full rent and three hundred of debt... I don't blame her. Her husband is out of town. She needs money too."

Rukhsaar broke down, her weary eyes gazed down, and her tears fell on the floor. "She said she will forgive the remaining money if we pack our bags and leave." she looked up at Masih, her face flooded with tears.

~

It was a bitter day. Masih kept gaping at her as she folded the plastic rug. Rukhsaar straightened her back to ease the burn in her spine.

My God, I don't want a cure; that seems too much to ask

91

for. Just allow me to ache in a way so he wouldn't know.

Rukhsaar covered their cup in plastic and threw it in a bigger bag beside the thermos, one stainless spoon, and a chipped plastic plate. She wrapped the brown plastic sheet on which they used to eat, and that was it. Rukhsaar piled all this and put it near the door, then gave the pillow and her sewing machine, which she had broken its handle a month ago, to Masih to carry.

Before they stepped out, someone knocked rapidly. Marzia was anxiously waiting on the other side.

"Just a few more seconds, we're leaving," Rukhsaar shrieked.

"Open the door!" Marzia cried out.

Masih looked at his mother, terrified of what's about to come. Rukhsaar put down all that she was carrying and opened the door.

Marzia was holding a plate filled with sweets, milk fudge, and cookies. Rukhsaar stared at Marzia's smiling face. She crept out.

"My beloved husband has returned today. Open your mouth!" She stuffed a milk fudge inside Rukhsaar's mouth.

"Where's Masih!?" She dashed inside and shoved Rukhsaar away.

Masih stepped backwards and bumped into the wall as Marzia ran towards him.

"No!" he cried, shielding his face.

"Open your mouth!" She threw his hands away and stuffed a jam cookie inside Masih's mouth.

Rukhsaar entered the room horrified. Masih almost burst into tears as he was choking and swallowing hard lumps of cookies.

Marzia proudly beamed at them. Rukhsaar finished her milk fudge and could finally speak. "What happened!?" she cried.

"Mujeeb *jan* arrived today! He had been promoted in his

business from fruits to expensive rugs. He will soon export them to Dubai!"

Rukhsaar inhaled.

Masih drank an entire glass of water.

"What happened? Why does the house look so empty?" Marzia asked.

"We were just leaving the house," Masih replied.

"What for?" she squealed.

"Because you said so!" Rukhsaar raised her voice.

"Oh, silly me. I completely forgot to tell you!" She chuckled.

"Mujeeb *jan* said you can stay here, it's okay. Whenever you had the money, you can pay us back."

She handed the plate with remaining sweets to Masih, who still had trouble breathing, then squeezed Rukhsaar's cheeks and left the house.

"What just happened?" Rukhsaar said and burst into laughter.

~

For the first time in ages, Masih saw her laugh. She was not covering her yellow-stained teeth with her scratched hands but opened her mouth in ecstasy and guffawed.

Her laugh sounded like a baby's giggle to Masih, like the ocean breeze. His spirit rose, it was badly contagious, but he stood still and watched her for a good while.

Eventually, they were going to pay for that smile painfully... so grant them to smile wider.

Chapter 20

Armed cradles

Happiness flooded around their little house. Rukhsaar started working again. The new pink pills were helping her. Masih asked what it was when she took two of them every night, but she said she didn't know the name and had borrowed them from teacher Noman's wife.

Rukhsaar also reminded Masih of school and assured him he will start next year since now the midterm exams had already passed, and he couldn't catch up. Masih had gone to the *madrasah* for his studies several times, but the rules had been changed, and now they only taught girls.

Their house levelled up as well. Marzia changed the look of her home for Eid, arriving soon after Ramadan, and gave her old drapes, the red rug, and three futons to Rukhsaar. Not just that, but Masih was allowed to watch TV once a week in their home, only on Thursdays.

Rukhsaar bought a radio for the home. On the radio, they listened to Ahmad Zahir during power cuts. It was their best buddy in their suffocating nights.

It's the worst kind of nights... an emptiness within so dark like the room, dire and grumpy, exotic sighs, long hours, overburdening nights, I gawk at the dead bulb. I wonder when it might light up, I can't help but imagine it lighting up the room's white walls. The radio would glimmer, and so will the sparkling red cushions.

The radio was the most important thing in the house. The

vital news at six pm and Masih's favourite drama shows at ten were their priorities. It was sacred and carried with extreme caution. Once Masih took it outside with him to enjoy a little fresh air, they treated it as family.

"Tomorrow is the first day of Ramadan," Masih said, then cleared his throat.

"Yes?" Rukhsaar smiled, folding the clothes she washed that morning.

"You promised me once I'm eleven, I can fast," Masih squealed.

"Only Fridays."

"But mother! I'm a big boy now," he cried, looking up.

"I said what I said... there will be a lot of Ramadans to come for you, don't worry."

Masih sighed.

"Masih?"

"Yes..." he said grumpily.

"We should go and buy some groceries today. I have saved a hundred Afghani," she said, lowering her voice.

"I'm not going with you..." Masih said, averting his gaze.

"I'll buy you ice cream..."

~

They were on the streets making their way through the hand carts, the anxious mob preparing for Ramadan, and plenty of traffic. Masih waited for his mother to finish so he could finally have the reward for carrying all her bags.

"Mother, why... why do they? I mean, why these men stare at you like that? You're in a *chadari*, but they still don't avert their gaze?"

"It doesn't matter if it's a naked body or women wrapped in *chadari* if it's their eyes that have no veil."

The sun was blazing that day, likely weather near Ramadan. A group of women were coming across Masih and Rukhsaar as they moved forward.

"Mother..."

"I know. Keep your head down and keep moving. I don't know her."

Jamila looked at Rukhsaar passing beside them along with her obnoxious in-laws, who were laughing. One of them glanced at Rukhsaar from the corner of her eye. She whispered something to Jamila and opened her purse.

"Wait!" the lady wearing a black abaya called.

Rukhsaar turned.

"Here." She stretched her hand, which carried twenty Afghani.

Rukhsaar glared at Jamila, who gazed down, she braced Masih, and they kept going their way without looking back.

"What an ungrateful bitch! We all know what you wanted to do with Jamila's husband, you slut!" and the group of women began cackling.

Neither mentioned the incident later. Masih enjoyed his ice cream, and his mother seemed apathetic, a sense of nothingness.

~

"Masih!"

Both spun to see who called. It was Masih's uncle.

Rukhsaar looked at Masih, whose hands quivered. He gulped and hid behind Rukhsaar.

She turned to disappear amidst the crowd, Razaaq called again. "Wait! They brought his body last Friday."

The bags fell from their hands, and the groceries spread all over the ground.

Rukhsaar slowly swivelled around, her eyes watered.

"He died..." Razaaq muttered.

"How!" Masih asked.

"In the middle of a war. He was martyred."

Razaaq yanked the grips of his handcart replenished with fresh cabbages he was selling and went on his way.

"Just like in the movies..." Masih muttered and at that

moment felt Rukhsaar's hefty hands over his face. He moved back.

"Your father died! You became an orphan! And that's all you have to say!" she screamed and ran the streets crying.

Masih halted, the people glared at him, some laughed, some snatched what fell on the ground, a man looked confused as to what the hell was going on between them. Yet, they all continued what they were doing. It wasn't about them, so it didn't matter at all.

Masih moved his hands away from his face and saw Rukhsaar disappear into one of the streets he had no idea where it led to.

The moment he turned his back on her, he heard a sound, a familiar voice.

The one that brought breaking headlines afterwards, red highlights. The footage in which a woman was raising herself and striking the ground, her hands surly uncontrolled, then she fainted.

A man whose boldface crinkled as he broke down in front of the camera. The children clenched garlanded pictures while gazing at the screen for sympathy. Yet, they didn't know what they wanted anymore since what they had and loved the most was already taken in such a way it was impossible to bring them back. They merely practiced anagapesis for their remaining days.

The news that left no one untouched, no family wary, no mother safe from grief, no father a masculine, and no children, children anymore. The news left them thinking peace was too much to ask for, or maybe now they were used to being blown away. After all, for a lifetime, gunshots had been their lullaby, the missiles their waking alarm, sleeping in armed cradles.

Chapter 21

Eclipse

Someone knocked on the door six times.

"It's them! They came!" two little boys standing beside Jamila shouted as they jumped.

Their mother, Shakeela, pulled them down.

"Shut up!" Sonya hissed.

"Should we open?" Shakeela asked her.

"I don't know... they did what they said they would do," Sonya whispered back.

"Was it six times?" Sonya asked Rukhsaar, but Rukhsaar looked away sourly.

Sonya sighed, glancing at Shakeela and said, "We are trying to find something to eat, and she is pissed because of some bloody cats!"

"Shush... don't say that she's sad, Sonya...it's what she loves. She spent so much time raising them..."

"She should grow up, Shakeela... I can't with this obsession of hers. She will get married one day. She can't live like this!"

"I'm not!" Rukhsaar jumped to her feet.

"That's not what I'm going to do! I'll become a veterinarian and gather all the street cats! They are homeless! They are dying under missiles!"

"So are we, Rukhsaar!" Sonya screamed, then hurried and opened the door that was being brutally thumped.

"What took you so long? I thought you died!" Fardin boomed.

"Is this all you could bring?" she asked, taking the plastic bags from Fardin, who was covered in sweat and dirt, his hair frizzier than it had ever been.

"What do you expect, woman? We stood in a queue the entire day!" He looked at his neighbour's kids and Rukhsaar sitting at the end of the basement, ogling at him.

"He is right, sister. Things have gone out of hand... Did you hear what happened in *Macroyan* today, with the girls?" the man standing beside Fardin said, lowering his voice, his appearance as horrible as Fardin.

"No, what happened, Hamza?" Shakeela stood beside Sonya and entered the conversation.

"It's good that we have some bread left because of Doctor Najib..." Fardin raised his voice, tilting his head towards the kids who were all eyes on them.

"Oh, yes, yes... ahem," Hamza said, nodding.

"Only bread?" the two minor twins asked at once.

"It's just for tonight. We'll find something better tomorrow," Fardin said, sprawling on the hard floor.

"I'm so tired, Shakeela!" Hamza said to his wife while stretching his aching legs.

The kids gathered. The bag contained two loaves of *ceelo* — round-shaped bread.

Sonya looked at Fardin.

"This is all we could get. Most of the families only got one..."

Shakeela cut each loaf into four pieces. The kids had the ones larger; Fardin and Hamza were apparently not hungry.

"Do you have any idea what the time is?" Sonya asked, sitting beside Fardin, clenching her expanded belly.

"How can I know...when we reached there, it was four pm," Fardin replied. "Are you alright?" he added, glancing at her pale face.

"I'm alright, just a little dizzy. Fardin, something tells me... I don't think I can make it..." her eyes began to water.

"Shush... you will. We all will, so will our triplets on their way. Don't say these stupid things again."

"I don't know..." she sighed.

"How is Rukhsaar?" Fardin asked, looking at his daughter huddled in a corner and gazing down at her feet.

Jamila slept beside her two little brothers. Hamza and Shakeela were having a private conversation in the other corner.

"You can see how she is..."

"She looks terrible," Fardin said, gawking at her. "My poor girl," he added.

"She can't live on like this Fardin, something should've happened. She can't daydream forever."

"I'd prefer daydreaming over this life we are now living," Fardin muttered.

"We have lived our lives, she must learn to live hers, and that can't be possible if she keeps collecting cats," Sonya hissed.

"She wanted that as long as I can remember, she wanted to be their fighter, but I heaved her and threw her in this prison while she was weeping over them."

"What else could we do, Fardin? It's better if she doesn't see them starving to death."

"Do you think they will make it?" he asked.

"I don't know. She put them in a small, poked cardboard under her bed with some water. They are smart. Perhaps they'll manage to live."

"I saw horrible things today .... "Fardin looked at her.

"What?"

"I saw them jump... I saw them throwing themselves from the *Macroyan* buildings in fear of getting molested by those bloody beasts." Fardin covered his face with his hands. His hands trembled.

"One seemed just twelve or something, she was holding her sister's hand as they were about to jump from the seventh floor, I saw them shattering... When did we get here?" he whimpered.

Sonya rubbed his back and wept.

"The bridge has been destroyed...people are dying from hunger and cold... Doctor Najib's aiding food has been finished—" Fardin cried hopelessly.

"Is he out yet?" she asked, cutting him off.

"He's still... he's still locked up," Fardin replied, covering his face and added, "Death must be laughing at how life is making us weep."

They were silent, yet it was not silence at all.

A deep growl, a leaden blast, ear-piercing whistles, gunshots sprinkled constantly, missiles crashed around now and then. Who was to say it won't hit their home any time soon? Collapse their house into pieces, then they'll be stuck in the basement.

The scenario played in each one's head. Sonya chanted prayers, crying one second, then smiling the next as she stared at the wall. It was strange how the human mind couldn't cope with disarray, so it fooled them with the memories, and with the help of the memories, they survived the night.

~

The war wasn't that heated. It used to be mild in the early mornings as if it were over. It would give them a little hope, thinking perhaps it was done, lying to themselves to feel slightly better, to grin and pretend it was normal again, to have a will to live and something to look forward to.

Fardin opened the basement door, all smiles. He ascended the stairs, burst open the jammed door by kicking it three times, and entered the garden.

He descended a step, his face changed 180 degrees, took his wife's hand, and helped her to climb. When they reached the lawn, they could see why that long face, they froze and observed.

The destruction inside the house could be seen through the large holes. Walls were crumbling, and the paint was falling off.

Fardin sat over the dead trees that he spent years nourishing. He drew his fingers over its branches; the trunks were shattered in half, roses merged with dust and spent rounds.

Was it really our home before? It doesn't seem like that at all.

"I'll go and take out the important things..." Fardin took a step forward.

"Hands up! I said stop and hands up!"

Fardin gasped and turned. He threw his hands behind his neck.

The rest gathered near the basement's door. Shakeela rubbed Sonya's wrist after she fainted and fell over in Rukhsaar's lap.

The two men who had their faces covered with black masks pointed their guns at them, their fingers clasped on the trigger.

"Get out of the way!" one screamed gravely.

Fardin nodded and stepped aside. He sprawled on the ground, gaped at his dead flowers. He chuckled, shaking his head, and hummed a song. Wild shattering noises were coming from Hamza's house as well.

آے شب تو بہت سے میرے دن کی دارہ دین
ہاں میرا دل تنتے آگ

He continued singing, "O Night, you resemble my days, Lord, my heart is agitated and unrested."

He nodded and watched the thieves taking out everything held memories—their TV on which they used to see classic Bollywood movies every Friday night.

"Don't forget the cassettes!" he called to them.

They stopped, glanced at him strangely, then carried on. Fardin didn't dare look at his left side, where his family was falling apart. He looked forward.

They took out the barrels filled with salted rice Sonya had been saving for years. Then their golden teapot which was delicately designed with liquid gold. He brought it last year from Russia for Sonya, a gift for their sixteenth anniversary.

Sonya touched it every morning as one would caress their infant; she loved it. God knew what her expressions were when she saw them taking it out that recklessly, it jerked against the wall two times.

Now it was time for his harmonium, on which he played his favourite songs when he was stressed or when they had memorable parties. Hamza would play his tabla, its rich drum sound accompanied Fardin on his harmonium, and they would sing together. They would sing songs, their eyes closed, sentiments at their best.

Fardin stretched out his hand towards it. They pointed the gun at him. Fardin pressed his hands together in front of them, pleading. "Just one last touch, please..."

The masked men exchanged glances and drew it slightly closer to him. Fardin tasked his trembling hands and touched its tiles softly, then let it go.

After that, it was time for something the burglars carried out in repulsion as if they were touching the filthiest thing to exist. The one carrying it threw it over the trees and went back indoors. After that, a faint sequel came through.

"Look, another one!" one of them shouted from inside.

"This one is alive!" he added.

"Let it get out, and if it's resisting, then shoot it."

"No! No!" Rukhsaar leapt forward, cried, and fell to her knees.

Shakeela pulled her back, moaning.

They heard a faint meow, then Jimmy stepped out, reeling with its broken leg. He saw Rukhsaar at first glance but refused to come forward to her. He averted his eyes from her to the trees and the white body lying over it. Jimmy stumbled towards it and placed his head near her paws, Mary.

The two burglars said something to each other and pointed the gun at them.

"What are you waiting for? Now get out of here if you want to live."

"I'm quite not sure if I want to...but I'll live for them," Fardin muttered.

"Get out!"

Fardin drew his lower lip between his teeth and stood up, clenching the nearby wall. He helped his wife stand, and they left their home as if they never lived there before. Fardin kissed the gate farewell.

Sonya covered her nose with her hands. The kids gagged because of the pungent smell of death... Dead bodies were lying around like pieces of meat, and the street rills that once carried melted snow was now still and scarlet. No home was left untouched; the same kinds of holes besieged each, some collapsed, some were still standing.

~

The path was more like a war zone than a pathway. Well, it was, after all, a war zone now. They walked faster when it heated up again. This time, tanks were rolling around. Young boys drove them.

"What are you holding? Why are you carrying your savings? You should save your life!" cried an elderly woman running beside Jamila.

"Nothing, it's nothing..." said Jamila as she clasped that box-looking figure close to her heart.

Jamila carried Holy Quran.

"But aren't we being called atheist Communists? The lady cried her heart out bitterly while covering her face.

Jamila peeked back. The lady was shot down, slumped in the middle of the street, her blood going cold like the little boy wearing blue shorts who collapsed beside her.

"It's alright, Jamila, keep running!" Hamza threw his hands over her shoulder as she wailed.

A large throng of homeless people gathered on the streets,

and everyone marched forward. Bombs exploded behind them. Rockets flew over them and crashed a meter away.

Their way got blocked by a tank. It slowly turned and pointed straight at them.

Sonya started wheezing. Fardin held her hand firmly. Hamza pulled his little boys closer to him. Rukhsaar and Jamila clasped each other's hands, they closed their eyes. Was this it?

"Please!" Shakeela cried, looking at the young boy's blue eyes, who held onto the tank's steer.

"Get out of the way! Quickly! Or else I'll shoot!" the young boy took the opportunity to fasten his green bandage on his forehead.

The two families jumped out of the way and scooted forward.

"Why are people climbing *Aliabad* mountain?" Shakeela asked as they were heading towards it.

"The other side is *Kart-e-Parwan*. It's safer," Hamza replied.

"Fardin, I can't..." Sonya slipped her hand away from his. "Please leave me. You go with Rukhsaar." She bent down.

"No! Are you crazy? It's just this mountain...after we get through it, you know we'll be out of here in no time. We just have to get out of here...please."

She sat, touched the ground, and wept while looking at her daughter, scared to death.

"Mother, please..." Rukhsaar sobbed.

Sonya struggled to tell where she was putting her feet on as if she walked on air. Fardin was under her left and Rukhsaar under her right shoulder, carrying her up. Hamza was aiding his children and Shakeela.

Flocks of families were climbing up that mountain. From afar, they looked like trails of little ants.

They reached the top and were catching their breaths. Was it all a lie? Nothing was happening there, tranquil, wonderful, yet what a tragedy, if only they knew what was about to come.

Sonya slowly sat on the ground, getting back to her consciousness. A woman approached them. She handed Sonya a bottle of water and the kids' packets of biscuits and left as promptly as she could. They got busy eating, and when they glanced back, she had vanished.

"Let's stay here for the night. The kids are weary; I can't climb down either..." Sonya said, gazing at Fardin.

Fardin nodded.

Another family stayed too. They were at the other end, too afraid to come close. Who knew who was whom? What were their true intentions? Who to trust anymore when there has been so much betrayal? When your own country betrayed you, there was nothing else left to trust anymore.

Her snores voiced in a rhythm. Fardin lay underneath her feet. The twins wrapped around Shakeela were in sound sleep as well.

Hamza lay cast away from them. Jamila lay her head over Rukhsaar's shoulder as she talked about the volleyball match, they were supposed to have that day. Rukhsaar stared at the eclipsed moon, fidgeting with her silver ring.

~

The climbing down was easier than they foresaw, and to their surprise, and the people on the other side of the mountain, *Karte Parwan*, were amicable.

A *kebabi* was fanning the kebabs and called people to come inside the restaurant. Hamza and Fardin decided to go in.

The restaurant's TV was on but was glitching.

It was old footage of when it started getting worse. President Doctor Najib was giving his condolences in the Kabul University regarding the collision of missiles. He cried, reciting verses of the Holy Quran, and called them to

stop this slaughterhouse and come to peace.

This attack had taken the lives of seven young pupils from agriculture, engineering, and other departments. Students in black were gathered across Mr President as they stood united and mourned their losses. Most of them probably dead by that day after the countless assaults that followed.

The kebabs would melt in their mouths with every bite. They savoured it, and to compliment the meal, they were served sour grape sauce that was too tart for Sonya, and freshly baked tortillas smelled like raw dough, which they all adored.

Fardin inhaled, glaring at the delighted faces of his family. He was seated beside his wife and across Hamza and Shakeela with the kids.

A man wearing black glasses approached him. Fardin appeared to have recognised him in a second and stood up. They shook hands. Fardin glanced at the table and left to the corner of the restaurant with the man.

Fardin's hands were folded. The man would peep around as they were having a watchful conversation.

"He came to our home a lot these days...Fardin knows him," Sonya said to Shakeela.

Shakeela nodded.

"Isn't he the one who works with the Soviets?" Hamza asked her.

"Shush...someone will listen! Yes, he is." Sonya answered, taking a bite of her food.

"So, there must be a lot of them he knows...I presume they came to your house as well..." Hamza said, looking outside through the window, a man parked his car.

"Who?" Sonya asked, her mouth stuffed with naan.

"The member of the Soviets..." he said, then yawned.

"Well, they did in the past, but obviously not now, plus..."

Fardin was back. He peeked around and sat with his family. He leaned forward. "This is it. He is the guy I told you about, Hamza; it's going to happen today *Insha'Allah*," Fardin said, his pupils expanded.

Hamza pushed the salt and pepper shakers aside. "Do you know the people going?" Hamza said, shaking his legs.

"No, who cares!" Fardin raised his voice. He looked back then sighed.

"There can be foreigners..." Hamza said, scratching the nape of his neck.

"Maybe...don't worry Hamza, nothing will happen; we're going to cross the border at no time. No one knows except for the embassy clients. It's just you who I've told because you're more than a brother to me. You know that, right?"

"Damn it! I'm just going to say it! I'm scared, Fardin...I can't risk my children's life. I'm scared of getting hit by a missile on my head by those bloody...!"

Fardin grinned at the twins, trying to distract them from what their father said aloud. The twins had their eyes widened at him. Fardin stared at Hamza.

"I'm sorry, Fardin." Hamza stood up.

"Hamza, maybe he is right. What else can we do? Let's go with them. Fardin brother is right," Shakeela said, looking up at him.

"Are you my wife or not?" Hamza asked her.

"What are you saying, Hamza?"

"Are you or not!"

The room gave them an odd stare.

"Of course, I am please talk slowly." she lowered her brittle voice.

"Then stand up!" he boomed.

Shakeela gazed at Sonya. Their eyes teared up. She clenched her twin's hands.

"Shakeela!" Hamza roared.

Jamila let go of Rukhsaar's hand and left without looking at her.

They both were tearing up. Rukhsaar gazed down. Tears dropped over the table as if she knew this was it.

"But we talked about this..." Fardin muttered.

"I can't, Fardin, we are going somewhere else," Hamza said, his back turned to Fardin.

"Where?" Fardin asked.

"I can't tell you."

"Where can be better than abroad?"

"You won't understand..."

Hamza left, not looking back once. Shakeela, however, had her troubled eyes on them till they stepped out from the restaurant.

Fardin slammed the table. A waiter approached them.

"Is everything alright? What are you doing?"

Their table started shaking, the floor vibrated, a flashy whistle then booms. The scenic frame of the Buddha in Bamyan fell and broke, glass shattered.

Fardin held Sonya's hand and escaped the restaurant, making their way through the crowd and debris.

None could see clearly. They would just run. The tanks were now on this side of the city as well, shooting around, destroying, leaving no spot untouched.

A crammed taxi approached them. A young man was lying on top of it, holding on to its edges to not fall. Still, it stopped for them. Fardin gestured them to leave, screaming, "Thank you!"

They ran inside a shop when a tank started running over people.

The shopkeeper locked the door, looking apprehensively outside.

He screamed and pulled down the window blinds. A scenario the heart couldn't take to witness.

"Thank you! Thank you for letting us in!" Fardin panted; his hands were pressed together.

The shopkeeper shook his head. "I've done nothing, you can stay as long as you want, but if you want to live, and your wife must be taken to a safer place immediately, I will suggest you leave this area."

"We're leaving today. I just need to get somewhere."

"Where?"

"Someone is waiting for us in *Shaar*."
The man paused and said, "I have a car..."

~

Rukhsaar had her head down, and her hands were cupped over her head. That was what Fardin instructed her to do. Sonya was crouched beside her, doing the same thing.

Fardin and the shopkeeper were at the front seat of the car. The man was driving, turning, bumping, and driving over dead bodies, fallen weapons, and collapsed walls.

Rukhsaar couldn't feel her back. Her legs were cold, and her hands hurt. Sonya had it worse than her. After an hour of unforgiving torture, the unsteady blue car finally stopped.

"Can I sit?" Sonya asked, her head still hanging down over her lap.

"Yes, yes." Fardin jumped out of the car and opened the door for them.

Rukhsaar stretched her back, and her bones crackled. Fardin swiftly aided Sonya to step out too.

The man raised his hand, waved them goodbye, and left.

"God bless you!" Fardin screamed.

In a deserted field, enclosed by nothing but sand and rocks, they were wandering like lost passengers.

"Where are we? Where's that man you told us about?" Sonya asked nervously.

Fardin nodded while glancing around. "It should be here..." His hands were trembling. He rubbed his forehead and looked as if contemplating which way to go.

"Look!" Rukhsaar beamed.

A black van came near them. It stopped beside them, and the door opened automatically. The driver exited the vehicle and nodded at Fardin, and Fardin nodded back.

"Let's go." Fardin helped his wife to enter first, then Rukhsaar heaved her leg to reach it and entered.

Fardin looked around and got in. The door closed smoothly.

Inside, the van was larger than one could expect by observing from the outside. The arm rests were made from leather, and the headsets were pleasantly comfortable. Sonya beamed and said she could sleep while leaning against them. Rukhsaar sat across from her mother, and her father sat beside Sonya.

They ignored the people around them and looked at no one. It was Fardin's command.

The fancy van proceeded to move steadily as if it's running on air.

Each person inside stole glances, sceptical of each other's presence. Six families were inside, except for a woman sitting alone.

~

Fardin observed the woman covered in a sort of veil that appeared foreign to most. Her sitting alone was a threat to him since he couldn't tell if there was indeed a woman behind that blue veil.

He had his eyes fixed on her every move, which his wife found uncomfortably strange as she glared at him. He dismissed her concern and would not explain anything now. It was overwhelmingly intense.

It had been fifteen minutes since they entered the van. If things went as planned, three hours to Takhar and the private jet would be off to neighbouring countries then they'll immigrate to Russia. Fardin couldn't help but smile, thinking about surviving.

The van lurched, and they were thrown back. Fardin stretched his arms in front of Sonya to protect her. The van accelerated, bumped, and stopped harshly as the tires voiced a horrible squeaking sound.

Even though Fardin tried his best to save them from any harm, Rukhsaar's head whacked with the seat across her. Her forehead turned red and bumpy but wasn't bleeding.

Fardin raised himself from his seat to see what was going on. His anxious eyes were fixed on the woman and afterwards the driver.

The door burst with a heavy object, it opened, and the driver put his hands above his head. Fardin felt a cold sensation in his cramping stomach. "No... God, please no," he said under his breath.

Two men with green scarves tied around their foreheads entered the van, each clutched their rifle.

"Hands above your heads! Hands above your heads!" one screamed. The other examined each one inside the van, his eyes bold and black.

He passed beside Fardin. Fardin kept his hands shielded in front of his daughter as they all had their hands behind their heads.

He stepped back and stood in front of the veiled woman. He said something to her, and she shook her head. That continued for a few seconds until the man lost his temper and snatched away her veil. She fell onto her knees. Her blonde hair was tied in a messy bun.

"So, it was you behind this all, huh? Making them like yourself, taking them away, you disgusting *kafir*!"

Fardin recognised her right away. She was his manager in the embassy where he used to work.

She pleaded with the man holding the gun in Russian while looking up.

Blood splashed from her head, and she was down, her eyes wide open.

Fardin fell back on his seat, his ears rang, his eyes welled up as he gawked at the black floor.

He failed to hear anything, and when he could, Fardin jumped to his feet.

Sonya cried in pain and crawled. The passengers looked at them.

Fardin stood up.

"Please let us go, please. I need to take her to the hospital."

"Have you lost your mind? Why don't you ask help from your communist friend, huh?" he roared and moved the deceased woman's head with his foot.

"She's going to die...please, I won't tell anyone about anything. Please, we are going to die, anyway; just allow me to see my babies, for once." Fardin fell onto his knees, his hands pressed together.

"Does anyone know anything about this stuff? Any doctors or nurse?" the other one asked, pointing his gun. If one said, "Yes," he would shoot them right away.

They all shook their heads, their palms in front of their chests.

Sonya's loud screaming gave rise to a kid's cry. The man pulled her arm and threw her out of the van. Fardin and Rukhsaar ran after her.

They ran forward. Fardin had a peek to see who stood beside the van outside. He focused on him. He was staring back right into Fardin's eyes.

Fardin didn't want to believe it, he laughed. "No, I've gone mad..." he muttered.

Fardin left Sonya and Rukhsaar and ran back towards the van. When he got close enough, he stopped, looked at him as the man gazed back. This time there was no excuse.

Sonya moaned, Fardin rushed back to her. He and Rukhsaar aided her to stroll faster.

Fardin was making excuses for what he saw as a lie.

It can't be him. It can't be Hamza.

But it all started making sense to him as he recalled their political debates.

What happened to the rest in the van? Who knows...?

Sonya wasn't screaming anymore. Perhaps she couldn't anymore, her droopy eyes were closed, but her legs were moving forward.

Once they got out of the deserted area, Fardin stopped a

taxi that had space for two of them and sent Rukhsaar and Sonya to the nearest hospital that was still functioning.

The taxi took off, and Fardin strode to the hospital.

~

Fardin arrived at the hospital two hours later. The guards obstructed his way and said the patient he was asking for hadn't laboured yet.

He was sure there was a misunderstanding. It had been two hours since they should've arrived.

She's already holding our babies. Maybe she needs time to rest.

Half an hour passed, and he heard his name. "Who is Fardin? Is there any Fardin?" a woman shouted; her voice worn out.

"Yes! Yes!" He made his way through the mob and entered through the hospital's door.

"Come inside!" she screamed.

A man grabbed him from the back of his collar, screaming, "When are we supposed to go in! I've been waiting here more than you!"

Fardin threw the man's hands away, whisked in. His heart ached to see his awaiting triplets.

The nurse took him to the waiting hall.

Rukhsaar stood up crying, and they both hugged each other firmly.

"I'm her doctor," the woman waiting for him said quietly, her voice at its worst. It would force the one listening to clear their throats.

"She's not going to make it..." the doctor said quickly.

"What...what do you mean?"

"We have to start her operation as soon as possible."

"Then do it!"

"How can I tell you this... Brother, she's lost a lot of blood, and there's nothing we can do, the babies condition isn't normal either, they might be...it's what we will tell you later, but for now we want to let you know that if we don't start the operation, we will lose the mother and the babies and if we do, the babies will make it and there is a chance of her living."

"A chance? What do you mean a chance?"

"You know what I mean, brother, I'm sorry. We're starting the operation now." she left and went into the emergency room.

Fardin bumped with Rukhsaar as he subconsciously moved backwards. They both said nothing and sat on the broken white chairs.

Another hour passed, and there was no news. Although three nurses had run out and entered the emergency room. He was dying to know why.

The door opened, and the doctor stepped out beaming.

"The mother and the babies are alive, thank God —" the light bulbs glitched as they were rocking, Rukhsaar fell, Fardin covered his ears. The doctor ran back inside, a missile crashed in some part of the hospital.

Fardin jumped in ecstasy, they both heard her certainly, and he was sure after asking Rukhsaar three times what the doctor had said.

Once things settled down a bit, Fardin and Rukhsaar sat back. He shook his legs, Rukhsaar was chanting prayers.

The door opened once more, and the doctor's face teared up, her eyes gazing down.

Fardin tilted his head towards the doctor as he stood to his feet.

"What happened?"

Chapter 22

My retrouvaille, We'll reconcile

A gloomy path surrounded by cries of terrified children, fallen handcarts, and running humans heading in opposite directions thrust Masih right and left as he searched for his mother.

A cold fluid poured down from his arm, Masih rolled his sleeves. He was bleeding, his clothes had been ripped, and his forearm was seeping blood. The burning sensation urged him to clasp his arm.

Masih made his way through and was about to enter the street he saw his mother enter before the explosion, but a man dragged him away.

"Where do you think you're going!?" an officer screamed, clutching Masih's arm, making him ache more.

"Mother, my mother..." Masih gawked at the officer.

The man looked at his palms and saw blood after touching Masih's arm. "Get out of here now!" he roared.

"But my mother..."

"I said go! This isn't a safe place. It was a suicide bomber! Your mother will be somewhere. Go to a hospital. You're bleeding!"

A car passed by. The man stopped it and pulled Masih closer to it. He took out a card from his chest pocket and showed it to the driver. "I'm a military man. Allow this boy to go with you. Take him to a government hospital. You don't have to pay! Just take him out of here!"

The driver nodded. He opened the door for Masih, and they

took off.

Masih turned around. The street was turning smaller as he stared from the backseat of the car.

The car stopped fifteen-minute later in front of a hospital. The driver said nothing. Masih stepped out, and the car vanished. He hadn't seen those people near that street, or maybe he forgot to look at faces.

Hordes of fearful people surrounded the hospital. A woman wearing a black abaya glanced at Masih then averted her eyes filled with disappointment. She had her phone stuck to her ear. She cried and had a peek at every stretcher descending from the ambulance or some who were being carried by people. The humans lying on the stretchers all came off as similar, nothing like they used to be. It was just blood and meat and bones.

Masih opened his eyes. When had they closed?

He heaved himself up. A boy, the same as his age, lay on the same bed beside him. A woman sitting on the floor was holding the boy's hand. He was in a room filled with wounded lying on beds and families on the floor.

Masih's nose started itching uncomfortably, he raised his hand, and it felt heavier than before. He turned to his right. Masih found himself attached to one of those plastic bags he used to see in the movies. He forgot about his nose and was oddly mesmerised by the long wire attached to his arm; a strange liquid was merging with his body.

"Where's your mother?" the woman on the floor asked him after half an hour of silence and uncomfortable stares.

"I don't know...I don't know." Masih spoke plainly the second time.

"Working child?" She let out a faint sigh and chuckled. "They just know how to labour, nothing about raising and taking care of one..." she said, shaking her head.

Masih clenched his fist.

"My son was in school. He's a topper." she snuffed.

Masih moved his head to look at the other side, to the

windows.

Dear life, please make sense again...

It had been one hour since his serum finished, but he couldn't make himself call the nurse since he felt guilty for her. In all this time, she hadn't taken a one-second break. The only time she wasn't running around the room for patients was when she was needed in other wards. This time when she entered, she came straight towards Masih's bed.

"Yours finished, why didn't you call me?" she smiled at him.

Masih was in awe of her.

She detached him from the tubing and left to attend to the patient in the bed across his.

Masih stepped down from the bed and left the room on his own, smiling.

His heart needed a little kindness, just a little, and that cute smile was exactly enough to help him carry on.

He started from the first door to his left. Masih would sneak inside, have a swift look and leave before someone caught him. Once, he called a woman mother when he noticed a doctor staring at him from afar.

The woman didn't mind at all. Perhaps she thought he called her by mistake. Nonetheless, he felt no shame at all like kids would when they called their teachers mother. Every kid's most embarrassing moment started from that one.

But Masih didn't stop there, he nodded, glancing at the woman, and left as if she gave him a crucial duty.

Masih inhaled when he got out of the room. He stood at the end of the ward, in front of the last room. He entered, peered around, but saw nothing new, almost as if the same people were sitting on the floor in each room and the same patients were on the bed. One had his forearm over his eyes, one was shooing away the flies, one was munching on something, one was throwing up in a bucket that stained the white bedsheets.

As Masih was about to leave, his sharp gaze caught a

brown mini purse, identical to his mother's. His heart jerked, he touched it, there was a whoosh, and he was smacked on his head.

"Thief! You Thief! You steal even in the month of Ramadan! Shame on you!" the woman cried.

Masih ran out as fast as he could. He glanced back, but no one ran after him, and when he turned to look forward, he bumped into someone. Masih fell backwards, yet the person in front of him was standing straight. Masih looked up; it was the same doctor who had given him a stare earlier, he gulped.

Surprisingly, the doctor gave him a helping hand.

"What do you want, kid? I've been watching all your drama. It's been hours." He crossed his arms.

Masih felt his cheeks heat up. "I'm looking for my mother," Masih said, striving to sound sweet and innocent.

"What's her name?" he asked in his deep voice, which wasn't sweet at all.

Masih gazed up at him, "Rukhsaar."

"Was she injured in the attack today?"

"I don't know."

"Where was she when it happened?"

"I don't know that either."

"Well, you have to just wait then. Sit on a chair and behave, or else I'll call the guards on you."

Masih nodded and sat on one of the blue plastic chairs that lined up the hallway.

The chairs were taken and emptied several times throughout the day. Masih had his eyes fixed on the edge of the white tiles and was staring at a hazel ant. It bumped heads with the other ant, and both walked on their separate ways. *If only she didn't butthead with me every time... Maybe this wouldn't have happened, maybe we would be together. It's all her fault.*

"Masih!"

Masih looked in the direction of the voice. Marzia stumbled towards him. Her scarf slipped down from her head and

119

revealed her spiky hair as if she'd been electrified.

"What are you doing here!?" she asked.

"What does it look like?" Masih rolled his eyes when he looked back, but the ants had disappeared.

"What?" she asked, looked where he was looking, then shook her head. "Come!"

"Where?" he said, yawning.

"Your mother is in the other ward! Why do you think I'm here?"

~

They were on their way. His heart throbbed. He rehearsed questions he was dying to ask her though he wasn't sure if he wanted to know the answers.

Marzia, however, resumed talking about how the beans spread all over the kitchen floor when she heard about his mother and how her good old husband was saddened by the news, but at some point, she said something on point.

"She gave my home address to one of the hospital crew, and they came bringing the news."

Masih analysed this... *How come she didn't mention her own son? Does it mean she's still mad at me, so it is my fault? Father left to buy for me a TV, maybe he went in the red zones for more money and then he died now mother will die also because of me, why am I not dying?*

He stopped. "Is it necessary for me to go? Did she tell you to call me?"

Marzia's eyes widened. "What are you talking about? She has been crying for the whole day when we couldn't find you!"

"Did she ask you to bring me?"

"How could she know you were in here! Masih, shut up and keep going. I think you've hurt your head or something. Better get you checked as well." Marzia tsk-tsked.

Before getting in the room, he had a glimpse of his mother through the slit of the door. Rukhsaar had her head against the white tiles, the pillows were behind her back and couldn't reach her head, she was, after all, a tall woman, like a flower; his father used to compare her to roses.

She gaped through the window, which was to her left.

Masih gazed at her for a good while.

What if she says she doesn't want to see me anymore, and she disowns me then says I'm no longer her son?

So, he gazed at his mother, who was the most elegant woman to him, even the actress he loved couldn't compare to her angelic beauty.

Marzia opened the door.

"Masih! I finally found him after so much effort!" Marzia crisply credited herself; there had to be a part in which she was invariably the hero or else her sentences would be incomplete. However, Masih knew she came there for the bathrooms were cleaner. She said it herself along the way.

Rukhsaar was weeping, her arms opened, looking at Masih as he cautiously fell into her warm arms. He inhaled, hugged her tighter. What a relief.

She held him tightly and sobbed.

"Where were you all this time? You know how much worried I was!"

"You left me," Masih said softly.

"No, I didn't." Rukhsaar snuffed.

"Yes, you did."

"How can a mother leave her son?" she patted him on his back.

"Like Father left me..." he muttered.

She remained silent. Masih let go of her. He didn't want to come off as annoying and stupid like he always felt he did. His hands were ice-cold as he wiped his tears.

Some strange pillow supported her back. Masih had never seen anything like that. It had holes in it.

"What's that?" he asked, pointing at it.

Rukhsaar glanced at Marzia. "For my back," she said softly,

touching it.

"But for what? Why?" he asked curiously, not wanting to touch it; perhaps it would make her upset, and she would leave.

"The doctors think it's necessary. I was in pain."

"Did you get hurt in the attack?" he yelped.

"No, no. Thankfully I didn't, but I lost control and fell, just like that day."

"Then take the pink pills, the ones that helped you before."

"They are furious I did that."

"Why?"

"They were right, Masih...I have a back problem." she sighed.

Masih wanted to ask what it meant but held his tongue.

"They said I should wait till the rest of the reports come back to see if medication is enough." Rukhsaar looked at Marzia. "May Allah be pleased with your *khala* Marzia. She paid for all the check-ups. We will be always in debt for the good they've done for us, remember that."

Marzia threw her hand, smirked, and couldn't help but get raised an inch, her shoulders pulled back.

"Where are the results?" Masih asked.

"They'll bring it tomorrow," Marzia said crisply.

"It's getting dark, Marzia. Take Masih with you to home. There is no need for you to be here."

"But...I can't leave you alone here! I just came..." Masih cried.

"There is no need for this, Masih. Sherin is alone at home. Her father left today. Marzia should go. It's getting late, and so should you."

"But..."

"No, Masih, leave. And as I told you, stop coming back." Rukhsaar peered at him.

Masih nodded rapidly before she became offended and left him in the middle of nowhere.

~

They stopped a taxi, and the sun had set before they reached home. Sherin, who was as sweet as her name, asked three times who was behind the door before she finally slit-opened it and fell into her mother's arms.

Masih smiled as both mother and daughter clutched each other firmly. He felt lousy for wanting Marzia to stay there with him, to keep him close to his mother while separating her from her daughter.

Marzia delivered him a bowl of rice with some beans and salad on top through Sherin to keep him replenished for the night.

He locked the door two times, like his mother would do every night, then covered the windows and when he wanted to turn off the lights, he couldn't make himself do it, so he left them on, didn't care if Sherin and Marzia judged him for fearing the dark.

It was hot under the blankets, too bright when they weren't covering his face. He raised his feet to put over Rukhsaar's body, but his feet hit the ground. His eyes welled up. He had promised Rukhsaar he won't cry but couldn't help it, so he sobbed. Tears rolled down from the corner of his eyes, wetting the hot pillow. He didn't care if Marzia and Sherin would hear him and laugh at him for sobbing under the blankets. He cried, his legs over a vacancy where once his mother laid.

Chapter 23

Troubled eyes

The files were over the table beside Rukhsaar's bed. Rukhsaar was gawking at the bed's iron bars above her feet when Marzia and Masih entered her room after dropping Sherin to school.

She blinked and simpered at Masih. He had his eyes fixed on the files.

"How are you feeling now?" Marzia asked, stepping closer to her.

"Better," Rukhsaar replied, her eyes fixed on Masih as if this version of her answer only related to him.

Marzia turned her back to Masih, they both did something in their sign language, and as Masih thought, he was kicked out politely from the room.

He didn't bother to protest, no more disappointment for his mother.

He sat on the blue plastic chair quietly. A man holding his crying baby asked Masih to bring him a bottle of water from the canteen.

~

"I'm not saying this to you for any more help Marzia, you have done more than I could ever ask for. I just told you the truth, so at least someone would know to tell him in the future."

"The cause, did they say why?" Marzia squealed.

"Razaaq...those bruises did more than just scarring into purple and blue." Rukhsaar looked at Marzia with an innocent gaze, and Marzia read her eyes.

"How much time...I mean—."

"Less than two weeks." Rukhsaar cut her off.

Marzia covered her mouth and bolted.

After an hour, Marzia exited the room, her face as grumpy as ever.

"You can go in. I'm going home. She will tell you what to do," Marzia said, and Masih nodded, looking at her perplexed.

He burst through the door and stood near the opening.

"Why are you standing there?" Rukhsaar asked, smiling at him.

"Can I come closer?" his voice broke off.

She opened her arms. "Come here."

Masih hugged her silently yet said everything he had in his mind. Perhaps she heard it too since she too was silent and held him longer than ever.

"Why did you ask me to get out of the room?" Masih asked, letting her go and sitting on the chair beside her.

"We wanted to have a woman talk... I can tell you what it was about if you really want to know..." Rukhsaar said, grinning.

"Mother! Tell me the truth!"

She twitched, and her face hardened. Masih had it worse than her. His heart shuddered; he clenched his sweaty palms.

Will she leave again?

"I have to stay in the hospital for about two more weeks..." she lowered her gaze.

"What!" he cried. This was worse than her leaving.

"I told them, but they're just not listening. More days is what they keep saying." she shook her head.

"What will happen after that?" Masih paused. "You will come back home, right?"

"Of course, my child."

"Then there will be no more pain?" Masih asked, and she nodded.

Masih sighed. He leaned back and tried to think about the

125

bright side.

"Why does it hurt, anyway?"

"Oh, it's because of the work and stuff, you know, until getting used to it. They said it's normal." Rukhsaar cleared her throat. "Now we need to get to the important things..."

He knew what was about to come, and he hated himself for knowing it.

~

Masih was in the taxi, looking through the window at the handcarts of fruits, markets, and tall buildings, the open sky, blissful families inside other cars.

The radio in the taxi was on. A presenter was speaking with the caller who chatted about one of his best memories, about jumping off a cliff and into a lake in Kandahar. But all Masih could think of was his mother's miserable words...

No more coming to the hospital till she was released to home. Not playing in the garden. Not getting out of the house at all, Marzia would bring him food. Not bugging Marzia to take him to the hospital because Rukhsaar had made sure Marzia wouldn't ever do that...

The car stopped, and both went to their separate homes.

Five minutes later, Marzia knocked on his door, gave him a plate of leftover rice from dinner, and said she would pick Sherin from school and go to her in-laws for *iftari*.

Masih locked the door after she left. He had a peek at the rice and its quantity was way more than his appetite, probably because that was for his dinner too.

The urge to ask Marzia if he could have their keys to watch TV lingered at the top of his tongue, yet he failed to confess it.

She would go crazy for sure or, even worse, accuse him of stealing. His mother wouldn't show her face to him ever again.

For five minutes, he tolerated the walls, the ceiling, as he lay in the middle of the room watching the red curtains and its crystals dangling from its edges. He sipped water then hastily sat up because he heard yesterday that it was *sunnah* to drink water while sitting. Rukhsaar always said to him to sit or else he'd choke and die.

He used the bathroom three times, and that was it. It was unthinkable for him to stay inside any longer. Just in the garden, no one will know.

He opened the squeaking door, circled the twelve-meter mini garden, and had three figs. He didn't bother to wash them.

"They're cleaner than my face," he said.

He sat on the grass, and his mind drifted to strange thoughts: a tremendous car, the colour must be red because it was his favourite, it would be the fastest car to exist in the entire world. Then its tires went flat, so did its top and gradually changed into a gigantic fish, a magnificent fish, its body made from coloured shells swimming in the blues.

He got struck by an idea, and the fish, poof, disappeared.

Masih jumped to his feet. He rubbed his eyes to adjust since they were busy gaping at the fluffy clouds for more than half an hour.

His evil mind resisted the dangers, giving him all the reasons why he was so dumb to stay.

How can she possibly know...?

He ran inside his home and looked at the wall clock, three thirty-three to be exact.

He ran back to the middle of the lawn, his hands on his hips.

The Maghreb is at seven, so she's coming after it... Till eight, they'll barely be finished with breaking their fast... One hour for fruits... she has a lot of information to give this time, so at least one more hour for chit-chatting and her unforgiving gossips. She'll hardly come back at ten pm! I'll be home in at least five. I'm doing it!

His jaw dropped. Marzia had taken the gate's keys with her.... he can't leave the house unlocked and leave... or can he?

Again, he put his hands on his hips, brainstorming.

127

Masih snapped his fingers, ran into the shed at the corner of the lawn where Marzia put the winter burning woods and her heaters and stuff. After ten minutes of rummaging, he ran back out, coated with sawdust while carrying a tall stool. He put it across the mucky wall that was about six feet high.

He looked at his reflection in the window and scrunched up his face. Masih got off the stool and ran to the well and poured water all over himself from the little blue bucket next to it. He peered around then took off his clothes completely. He grabbed the white soap beside the well from inside a pink soapbox. Used the same soap for his spiky hair, hardened with sweat and dirt.

He soaped his hair three times until it was at last gunk free. He ran into his house naked. Masih pulled out his bundle of clothes from underneath their table and unwrapped the green square cloth wrapper and took out his brown t-shirt and trousers. He was looking like a million bucks by the time he got dressed. Now, the ugly slippers won't match his look, so he took his shot and wore Sherin's black sneakers, which were across their home's doorway. It fit him perfectly. "Sorry, Sherin..." he muttered, tying its laces.

Masih climbed the stool, it reeled, and he instantly gripped the top of the wall. He heaved his right foot and bent the other, jumped on the wall, and glanced down the street. The wall came up way higher than he anticipated. He took a deep breath.

"You're the *bache film*, Masih. You can do it better than Tom Cruise."

The scene where Tom Cruise jumped down from a helicopter continued to play in the back of his head. He had seen it on a store's TV, but the shopkeeper shooed him away before he saw how it ended.

Masih sat on the wall. His feet were swinging loosely. He slowly let himself down and stood on his feet after the safe jump.

He tucked his clothes in, all smiles.

The ice cream seller's soft symphony was music to his years. He couldn't help himself. He took out his hundred Afghani and bought his favourite flavour, the sour orange one. He counted the change and put it safely in his pocket.

The sun was lightly obscured by the mists; however, this time, he had no time to see what shapes they were making, so he went on, licking the popsicle.

He had to pass in front of his boss to reach where he was headed, so he bought a facemask from the pharmacy.

There was no chance of him being recognised now, looking all dashing like that. Who would've thought he was an *esfandi*, a shoe polisher? No one! And he liked it, this new Masih, the cool one, new shoes, new style, new him, even if it was for a day, it was okay. He was sick of the old Masih with his heavy baggage.

He planned to see his mother in the hospital, but after ambling on the streets where she left him bamboozled, he decided not to.

He'd rather travel around his little world, not believing in borders. For him, it was a free world.

Masih was on his way back home. The popsicle finished, so did the urge to be this new kid. He couldn't be new when he still carried an old past and a rusting present.

How can I be new again?

While coming towards home through the treeline street, his eyes caught people standing near their gate. Masih ran to them. A boy attempted to climb up their wall as two other men were raising him.

Masih looked at the crowd. Mujeeb was sitting on a block of stone, pulling his suitcase closer to himself, and then Mujeeb covered his face with his hands.

Marzia and Sherin were holding hands and nervously looking at the boy who was now on top of the wall and wanted to jump in their yard.

Sherin covered her eyes with her hands as the boy jumped,

a thumping sound, footsteps, then the clicking of the gate, and voila, it opened by the boy wearing a prideful grin.

"Here he is!" the boy standing in the doorway screamed, his finger was pointed at Masih.

Masih gazed at Marzia, her chest puffed, her eyes squinting, and her face was turning purple.

She took a step forward, but Mujeeb pulled her back. Marzia and Sherin went inside, and the folks disappeared muttering.

Mujeeb approached Masih. His heart was about to stop any second now. Masih lowered his gaze and gulped in terror.

"I wasn't expecting this from you, Masih..." Mujeeb said and walked inside.

Masih wished he slapped and beat him to death than having Mujeeb kill him with this shame.

He ran inside his home and locked the doors before Marzia came to murder him.

"But she had said she's coming after *iftari*!" he cried to the walls and smacked his head when he realised Mujeeb arrived today from Dubai.

"My cursed luck!"

Someone gently knocked on the door. Masih noticed from her tall and skinny shadow fallen on the ground it was Marzia. He held his breath.

"I know you're inside, Masih!" she yelled, knocking harsher with her fist.

A small, tinted window in the kitchen faced the street, it could be a fair escape, but for that, he needed to rip off its grating. He thought about the bathroom window, though it was near the ceiling, and to reach it, he needed the stool which had collapsed on the lawn thanks to him.

It started to feel even worse than the day he had to escape Gul.

Why am I always running away from people!

"I've brought you food!" she yelled.

Masih slowly pushed aside the blinds and saw the plate of

grilled potatoes she was carrying with naan on top of it. He inhaled the scent of fresh bread coming through the window and saw its steam rising high. "I... I don't trust you. You're going to hit me!" he cried.

Marzia sighed and muttered something. She left, and a few seconds later, Sherin came knocking on his door, holding the plate. Masih peered closely around her to make sure Marzia was not sneaking behind the walls ready to attack him like a predator hunting her dinner.

He opened the door a slit.

"What are you doing, Masih? Open the door!" Sherin squealed.

He snatched the plate and closed the door.

"Sorry, it's because your mother scares me to death!" he yelled, locking the door.

Sherin shook her head and left for her home.

He carefully washed the plate to not break it. He already was in enough trouble.

This time she will leave me forever...

There was another knock on the door, precisely three times, soft and gentle.

It was someone new for sure. Even Sherin wasn't that diplomatic.

Masih opened the door. Mujeeb smiled at Masih as he looked at him from their see-through glass door.

He stood unmoving, ogling at Mujeeb.

"Ahem... won't you ask me to come in?"

"What? No, I mean yes, yes." Masih made way for him to get inside the room.

The six-foot-four Mujeeb was enormous for their tiny room. He came off as a giant in a Barbie doll's house. His head nearly hit the ceiling when he first stepped inside.

Mujeeb sat cross-legged on the futons, yes, futons, because he utilized two of them.

It was the first time Masih saw him for more than a minute,

so he took the chance to memorize him, his white sparkling teeth, his brunette hair richly oiled and brushed back neatly, a black mole on his left cheek and his infectious smile.

Masih failed to remember what his mother said about Mujeeb's birthplace.

The name... what was the name...?

Masih kept brainstorming while Mujeeb told him about a story when he lived the best time of his life in Bande-amir at Bamyan. He even promised Masih to take him there next year along with his best friends and colleagues who are from there. "Very sweet people they are!" Mujeeb beamed.

He spoke very politely, even though he had an accent when he spoke and would subconsciously switch to Pashto now and then.

Mujeeb is related to Marzia, so it is obvious he is also from where she is... Kunar is the province's name!

Masih stood up when Mujeeb finally stopped talking.

"What are you doing?"

"Bringing you some tea," Masih replied, heading to the kitchen.

He felt embarrassed making all the noises from the kitchen as he accidentally spread the spoons all over the floor. It clanged, hitting the cement. Masih turned his back to Mujeeb so he couldn't see him struggling through the thin curtain.

"You don't have to, son," he called on him.

"No, no, I have to. Mother always said... says to be hospitable. Offer your blood if there's nothing else you can serve them. They are the guests of God. That's what she used to say. So, I must, even if she's not here, it's my responsibility."

Masih brought a cup of leftover black tea from last night. He heated and poured it into their nickel thermos.

Two sour candies he borrowed from Mujeeb's own house lay beside the teacup.

Mujeeb took a sip and raised his eyebrows. "Very good, very good. *Aafarin* Masih *jan!*" he said, putting the cup down.

Masih wished he rather said it stinks because it was from last night than being this kind to him, his acting even more hilarious.

Now that he was used to the truth, even a slight compliment made him feel uncomfortable.

Mujeeb stood up abruptly. "So Masih *jan*, it was nice talking with you. I hope I didn't bug you too much or gave you a headache!?" He laughed.

Masih beamed, shaking his head.

"You don't have to be alone, don't ever feel like you're alone, son. You can always come and go in our home as you please. I've talked with Marzia, and Sherin would also love to play with you. I'm going back tomorrow. I came here to invite you for dinner at our home. Will be waiting for you, young man." He put his hands on Masih's shoulder and looked at him for more than a few seconds. The gaze was both sympathetic and scared.

His gaze being kind is obvious, but why so fearful?

Masih nodded, and Mujeeb left the room.

Masih forgot to close the door for a minute straight since he was busy gawking at the wall, remembering that gaze. Something wasn't right about it.

~

Even Sherin came off surprised to see Masih that innocent, sitting cross-legged, pulling out paper towels to wipe his mouth after every bite of the roasted chicken, gazing down, and the only words he said that night were yes and no to their questions, mostly Mujeeb's.

Marzia was washing the dishes in the kitchen. Sherin had fallen asleep while she and Masih were watching Tom and Jerry. Her head lay against the polished cabinet beside her.

Mujeeb was having a private conversation with Marzia standing near the kitchen's doorway when Masih yawned and stood up.

"Good night *khala jan* and *kaka jan*. I must go back home now," Masih said, standing away from them.

"Sure, but you can sleep here in the spare room if you'd like."

Marzia gave her husband the stare.

He didn't want to. He was exhausted by all this acting, after all.

"No, no, I'm comfortable in our room. Thank you for the dinner."

Mujeeb nodded, smiling at him.

Masih approached the hallway door and stepped out, then noticed he carried Sherin's science book all the way. He stepped back inside.

"Less than two weeks... that's shocking." Mujeeb sighed.

"Yes... and the amount they are asking for is even more shocking," Marzia squealed.

"How much was it again, thirty...?"

"Mmm, thirty thousand..."

"That's loads of money. Doesn't she have anyone... I mean, what type of tasteless people she's related to?"

"No one is willing to pay that much. Everyone has a life of their own, you know."

"Yeah... even I can't do much. I'm just standing on my feet."

"You don't worry about it Mujeeb, you did more than you should've already."

He sighed once more.

"I just feel awful for him. It's so hard for me to look him in the eyes... does he know?"

Marzia tsk-tsked.

The book fell from his hands, and they stopped talking. Before Mujeeb caught him, Masih ran to his home.

He locked the door, pulled the curtains, and didn't turn on the lights. He hunched in the corner.

About two weeks, less than two weeks, I have a mother,

then what? Why? What have I ever done? What's my sin that I can't be forgiven for... what have I ever done?

He didn't cry, he didn't speak a word, but he was crawling inside his skin, screaming within, hushed and gloaming, yet overwhelmingly obnoxious.

The dark erred to make him scared this time since now he had the scariest of lives.

Masih hurled himself and squeezed his torso against the wall behind him. His chest rose and fell; his arms were folded underneath his forehead as he gazed down at the flowers of the rug. The night ended, but it didn't feel like a day began. It had been all darkness since he heard that. He waited for Mujeeb to leave first, didn't want to disappoint the only one who happened to care.

Chapter 24

Forlorn

Marzia was in tears as she ran after Mujeeb. Her scarf slipped from her head, and she was carrying a glass of water. Mujeeb smiled at her, pulled her closer to him. He hugged her, and she wailed.

Mujeeb stepped outside and waved goodbye then Marzia poured the glass of water in his direction after he was out of sight. Masih watched them through the window.

He'd seen his mother doing it every single time his father left. She would fetch water and pour it after him. Masih asked her why and she said, "So he would come back to me as quickly as the water pours." She beamed, saying it to him and adored the glass of water by staring at it awestricken.

But why didn't the water bring him back? Or did she forgot to pour it the last time he left? The water... will it save Mujeeb the way it did his father last time? In a way, he wanted it to, so it wouldn't be hard to explain to Sherin what it was like to be him.

Marzia, at last, closed the gate and wiped her tears. She caught Masih staring, though Masih didn't bother to hide; nothing mattered anymore. She looked at him strangely and walked back to her home.

He heaved the rug and took his five hundred Afghani he'd been saving through these past months. He put the money in his pocket.

"Masih!" Marzia shouted as he was about to open the gate.

He ceased but refused to look back.

"Masih!" she called louder. "Your mother told you not to leave. You are my responsibility! I don't want trouble because of you," she cried.

"Sorry," he muttered and slammed the door shut as he left.

Tell my demons it's their turn to fear me. For now, seems like I fear nothing but being alive...

There was a relief in knowing he was not loved when there was nobody who cared enough.

Wild and vicious off he went.

Where to go?

The shoe polisher was the only person he could think of because again he had this urge of leaving, the ecstasy of escapism...running away from everything and everyone to a safe place. That man was the only one who kept him grounded. Perhaps this time, he would do it again. It was a matter of about two weeks after all.

"Do you think I'm a fool? You haven't come for a week! Get out of here!" the man roared, shooing him away.

"But I need the job. I need money. My mother is sick," Masih cried, dodging the man's massive hands.

The man stopped as if Masih just said the magic words, Mother...

"Mother, eh?"

"Yes..."

"Why would I trust you again?"

"Why would I come back?"

The man looked at him, sighed, and stepped down from the square stone. "Okay then, only for your mother. Mothers are a blessing; heavens lay under her feet."

Masih nodded, not sure what to feel since all he could think of was her living in hell with him, and she now abandoned him in hell as well. He couldn't see where the heavens laid.

"I'm going now. You better payback for all your absence. Work a lot today, got it?"

Masih nodded, even more unsettled than before. How could he pay him back? As if it was in his control to attract dirty shoes.

"Good." he left, throwing his black and white shawl over his shoulder.

One hour passed no one even bothered to stop by. His boss would be back in two more hours. A week... thirty thousand... More than a thousand a day.... thirty thousand all at once... somehow.

"Hey, kid! I'm talking to you!"

Masih averted his gaze from the box and looked up. An elderly man stood straight but was wearing slippers. He gawked at his feet then picked a soft brush. Maybe it could work. Masih brought the brush closer to the man's feet.

"What are you doing?" the old man shouted, pulling his feet away. "Do you want to force me to give you money?"

"What do you want?" Masih asked exasperated.

"Do you have change? I need two tens for a twenty. Hurry up, my grandchildren are waiting for their money." He pointed at two boys standing on the other side of the street. One of the boys stared at Masih.

Masih stared at him too.

"Do you have change or not?" the man yelled.

Masih sighed. "Tell your grandchild, Masih said hi."

"Who are you?" the man asked, looking at him from head to toe.

"Once his best friend, now he's too ashamed of me to come closer."

"My grandson can't be that filthy to be friends with a shoe polisher. I'm proud of his decision."

Masih smirked, putting down the brush. It was always your worst days when you got to know your worst bonding.

"Now, even if you do have the change, I don't want it. You disgust me." He left, lending Masih a ghastly stare.

Another hour, no one came. Maybe because he wasn't

screaming at the top of his lungs, calling the ones he caught with dirty shoes, but today was just not his day, and he couldn't care less. The thought that his boss will be back in an hour terrorised him, his throat choked up. He struggled to breathe.

The shopkeeper across the street who always had his eyes on Masih as if he were guarding a treasure box was nowhere to be seen today. Was it a good chance?

Is this it?

Masih, with the shortness of his breath, had a firm grip on the box. He stopped hearing the car honking, the bicycles ringing, the children running around, and the handcarts.

It was heavy though not heavier than what he had been carrying since last night. He got up, turned, and ran.

Just because Masih hadn't seen him in his shop didn't mean he wasn't there. Masih threw himself in every narrow street as the shopkeeper was after him, not after him, but after the treasure box. The man yelled vulgar curses.

I just heard him abusing my sister, my sister who doesn't even exist... I wonder what did she do, anyway? What was her fault? Why was she the one who had to be dragged, just because she is my sister? A sister I don't have was insulted. What do the ones who exist go through...?

For once, Masih looked back, and in that exact second, he bumped into someone and fell on his face. The footsteps behind him stopped. Masih's eyes were fixed on the dirtiest pair of shoes he had seen yet. It would take him three rounds to clean them up, but he wasn't there for that, nor was Masih fallen there to examine a man's shoes.

No one made a move which was making him crazy. Masih bent his arms, and his hands were scratched on the rough ground. He crept and slowly raised himself. The box remained by his feet, cracked from the left side, but still locked securely.

He couldn't find the audacity to pick up the box or look at the man he bumped into or the shopkeeper thirsty for his blood. All of them had something in common; all of them were enraged at Masih. The broken box because he broke it., the shopkeeper for betrayal, and the tall man in front of him for crashing into him.

Deep down, he feared when he looked up, he would see the man who took him to that office the other day.

But he looked up, and he wasn't that man, though Masih wished he were because this young boy was the same boy who he had seen standing in the yard when he escaped the 'office' and Gul. His dusty curls were fallen across his drowsy eyes, his clothes stained by blood. The white trousers of his *perahan tunban* were pulled up to his shins, and the hems were folded. He was someone whom Bibi *jan* would call a *dozd* and most likely an addict.

As Masih predicted, the boy took out a sharp knife from his pocket. He showed it to the shopkeeper and faded away. Masih visualized how it felt to be cut by that knife, to be stabbed.

Would it hurt more? Or he wouldn't feel if he thought about his mother.

He clenched the knife firmly between his peeling black and cracked nails.

Masih stood passive; he didn't want to survive this time, nor did he think he could.

The man behind him disappeared. The boy took a step back, raised his knife, drew his own thumb from its tip to the end of its sharp edge, and induced himself to bleed. Masih felt the chill in his spine and held his breath. The boy smirked and licked his thumb, then put back the knife in his pocket.

So, he wants to strangle me with his hands and sell my kidneys?

The boy turned his back to Masih, paused then took a step forward.

"You're not going to kill me?" Masih muttered.

The boy stopped, then kept wandering into the distance and turned to the narrow-left street.

~

"A thousand is my last word, kid, now give it to me or get out," a shopkeeper said, shooing Masih away.

He was a lanky man sitting on the other side of the glass table inside his shop. Masih, who was now used to getting shoved, ignored, and being something incogitant, looked at the man counting his money with the help of his salvia. He sighed and propped the box towards the man.

"Fine," Masih said.

The man picked a tattered thousand note and gave it to Masih. "Good choice. No one would buy stolen stuff from you anyway," he said, looking down at Masih; his glasses had fallen on his big nose.

Masih kept quiet and got out quickly.

How the hell do they know all about me? How do they know I'm not worth even being killed!

He thought about the boy.

How silly of me to think he'll kill me. Why would he? I'm just a waste anyway, a waste of space, a waste of time. Even in the movies, something happens. Maybe I was wrong; there is no plot twist; it's merely life.

Not being hurt by the boy to Masih was way worse than being dismissed like that. As Masih stepped out from the shop, and what he saw halted him. The same boy stood still across the door. He stared at the cash curled in Masih's fist. Masih stretched out his trembling hand and opened his hand. The boy took the thousand and limped away.

A lady threw a ten Afghani in front of Masih as she passed by. Masih was hunched near a girls' high school pathway. He stretched his hand and took the money.

What did I just do? Why did I give him my money? Why didn't I do something? I could've screamed. I could've run. Masih, what are you doing? You are supposed to save your mother...

The Mullah *sahib* preached the afternoon adhan from the mosque across him, which urged him to stop screaming at himself like a maniac.

It was her money, not mine.

Masih stood up and reached the shop in a few minutes.

He circled the area four times until the Mullah now preached the last adhan of the day. It was nine pm, and as much as he tried to not think about the dark, the more he felt its consuming presence in every gaze and even in himself. He found the gloom in the streetlights, in homes that gleamed with yellow lights, in the shops and their tube lights. It was dark in the stars and the full amber moon. It was the brightest kind of dark.

Masih went back to the bakery from where he bought naan, the five Afghani ones which are the leftover from the morning; the reason it was half the price. He ate it all yet tasted nothing. It was him, the inevitable gloom and a tasteless mouth.

"Are there any street dogs here? At night-time?" Masih asked the baker who locked his canteen and headed out.

"I don't know," he answered and was gone.

Masih wished the baker kept quiet and ignored his existence like everyone else passing by. Maybe that way, it would feel like a yes.

Life never felt so... dead, padar jan

Chapter 25

The Ally

His first thoughts in the morning were that it marked the second day, and he had earned nothing but a five hundred note he had saved before, and he was going to spend five Afghani for breakfast.

Masih stretched his arms and examined himself for a bruise or something, but he was safe and sound, so there were no stray dogs, but his wrists had never been this feeble.

People were already in lines to buy fresh naan. A man who bought one halved it and held it to Masih, who was going to buy from the hardened ones.

The man looked into Masih's eyes then tried to be kind, and it hurt, even more, to be understood like that.

Masih accepted the bread with a thank you. It was scalding hot, so he sat back and put the naan over his lap for it to cool down a bit. Its doughy aroma was incredibly tempting, so he did nibble on it now and then.

The five Afghani bought him a small packet of two wheat biscuits, enough to keep him company till night or maybe even till the next morning if he failed to find something to eat.

Once more, he was near the girls' high school, propped against its grey wall, underneath the shade of the trees that stood on the inside of the walls. He brainstormed about the seconds passing by, one week, thirty thousand, Mother.

One of those black mirrored cars caught his eye. It stopped near the school's gate. Its windows pulled down, and a young girl dressed in her school uniform stepped out of the car from the front seat and waved at the driver. He looked at his daughter smiling as she entered her school, then he averted his eyes to the steering wheel when he caught Masih staring at him.

A car passed, yet when the barrier persisted, they still looked at each other, examining the differences between them. Like those pictures of finding the difference, but this one had nothing in common.

To his surprise, instead of cursing, making a face, or ignoring him, the man got out of the car and approached Masih. He sat beside him on the footpath.

"Are you from the TV? Is this a movie shot?" Masih asked, looking around, feeling butterflies all around his cold stomach.

The man smirked, shaking his head. His eyes crinkled, and he drew his fingers through his silky grey hair. "No, no, I'm not an actor."

He hadn't mentioned, yet he already got what Masih meant, which struck Masih to feel even more decent about him.

"But I'm handsome, eh?" he said jokingly.

Masih forced a smile.

"So, your parents make you beg and work on the streets?"

He didn't know if he should say no... or say yes. She was making him, her cursed life which she had inherited was making him, his father going too soon was making him, them giving him birth was making him. He just looked at the sparrows that flew away from the orange fence.

"I like your shirt," the man said, looking at the words printed on it, 'To heal is to hurt.' He spoke in a sweet *Herati* accent.

"I don't have money..." Masih confessed out loud. "In case you were still wondering, look at me? Do I look rich to you?" Masih added and pointed at himself.

"What do you mean?" the man frowned.

"Why are you acting as if I have?"

"I'm just being me..." the man said, looking down.

"No, you're treating me as if my ripped clothes, dingy face, and muddy hands don't matter. You're being kind as if I have money, I can't do any good for you, I'm sorry. Go now."

"It doesn't matter to me, I'm just talking, but if you want, I can leave you alone."

Masih looked him in his grey eyes and shook his head gently.

"Do you know what it means?" he pointed at Masih's shirt.

"Yes...it's in French. You won't get it." Masih huffed and pulled his shoulders back.

The man cackled, and the baffled Masih looked at the man wiping his tears of laughter.

"I like you a lot!" He took out something from his chest pocket.

Masih pretended he was looking at the grass.

He put it beside Masih and stood up.

"Are you that rich?" Masih asked, looking at the thousand Afghani note.

"If pieces of paper known as money will entitle me to be known as 'rich'...then I'll rather be called poor for a hundred lifetime. Son, don't give it too much importance."

"What's your name?"

"Ayaar." He smiled and waved goodbye.

A thousand note... Yesterday, when the shopkeeper held him that note, it was the first time he saw it let alone own it, and five seconds later, he lost it. Now he had it again. This time the first thing Masih did was to buy a little plastic bag. He put his fifteen hundred inside it, then took out his right shoe, laid the plastic inside it, then put it on. There the money would be safe.

Masih let out a sigh of relief, but the lumps in his shoe were extremely uncomfortable, although after ambling around the area, he got used to it just like every other suffering.

He walked to the shop, near the school, at the bazaars, and the narrow streets he first bumped into him, but the boy was nowhere to be found. Masih came back to the shop and, this time went inside.

"What is it?" the thin man asked him, his attitude not the same as it was when Masih held the box. This time he had looked at Masih's empty hands.

"Yesterday, when I was just getting out of your shop, someone stole my thousand Afghani."

"You should've been careful. There's nothing I can do. Get out."

"I'm not asking you to do anything for me. He was tall, white, had curly bushy hair and drowsy eyes, and walked in an unstable motion."

"What? Do you want to take your money back from him?" the man asked jokingly.

"Yes," Masih replied; he had never been this serious.

The man paused organising the shoes on the shelves of his shop. "Are you out of your mind?"

"That was not my money. It belongs to someone else."

"Listen, kid, you have gone crazy, and I don't want to have any part at this. The things you said resemble an addict, so you might find him in *Zere-pul* (under the bridge) of *Pul-e-Sukhta*. Now leave my shop. You're blocking the way for any customers."

"Where is this place exactly?"

This question stuck with him as he followed wherever people sent him after giving him an odd stare. It wasn't like Masih didn't know about the stories of under the bridge, specifically by his best friend who said if someone once gets there, he might never make it out, although he couldn't care less and his best friend was quite dramatic, so he went on.

The journey to under the bridge cost him three hours of strolling on foot, a starving body, trembling feet, and a ten Afghani for a *bolani* since he was about to pass out.

He stood where people called it "River of Kabul." Did it look like a river? Absolutely not, nothing like a river, nothing like Kabul, more like a river of traumatizing junk, peels of fruits, tainted food, pampers, and all of this merged with humans covered in scarves at the corners of this cavern. Why did it get the name? Once upon a time, there was a river; like every other good thing, we lost it.

The pungent smell exhorted him to cover his mouth, but he stood miles away from where he needed to go.

So, this is under the bridge...?

He walked down, and no one paid attention to him, not even the traffic police, probably because he was actively screaming his heart out to a car that wanted to go, not one car, all of them wildly anxious to leave sooner than the other. With one hand, he would control the traffic, and with the other, the handcarts, the crowd, one human so many unsuccessful attempts.

It was quieter down there than the place he was looking down earlier.

Now instead of junk, another pungent smell allotted him a strong headache. Masih heaved his collar and covered his nose and mouth with it. He smelled the Surf Excel washing powder merged with his scent.

He stood in a place that, for the first time, he was the one giving others an odd stare but would get none of it back, or at least at this time. One man lay over rotten tomatoes as if they were flower beds. He faced the sky smiling; his eyes were closed. Two were busy sitting mouth to mouth to each other and were turning on a slightly burned red lighter as they began to breathe something Masih had never seen before.

Masih went there for someone, but he was now frightened as hell looking at all of them, at their urge to bring their hands to their noses and breathe then act as if they died.

For a second, Masih looked around to see if there were any cameras. He was being recorded for a scene, another scene of his wildlife. He wished someone would have recorded it or wrote about it, at least...

He didn't dare to get closer; he could smell them already

from afar, and all that dusky smoke shortened his breath. Only one man remained at the very end who seemed to not share whatever poison he was wielding. To go all the way there and not see that guy's face would be unacceptable, so Masih walked to the dead-end.

His heart skipped a beat when he saw all that money lying in front of the man; seven of those purple-coloured notes were spread out. Masih looked at the boy and recognized him immediately.

He bent and slowly leaned towards the money. The boy moaned, almost like he cried under that see-through black and white scarf covering his face. Masih gulped; his hands were trembling and levitating over the money. He stood straight. He looked at the boy one last time as now the boy crunched his torso into a ball and snarled.

Masih turned and faced the open way, like an aisle, but instead of chairs, he was surrounded by addicts.

"Why didn't you take the money?" His voice was gentle and smooth, unlike the way he presented himself. The voice was what gave Masih the audacity to face him again.

The boy's eyes weren't drowsy, they were wide open, and he slightly squinted to see Masih under the blazing sun.

"Why are you standing there like the Buddha statue?" The boy smirked, asking him.

"I didn't take my money because you disgust me, and you've touched that, so they are no longer clean."

"Oh...so the money was clean before? Really? All *halal* and your well-earned money, wasn't it?"

Masih felt a fervour flush burning his face.

The boy jumped to his feet. "Run! Run!" he cried to his fellow citizens who were about to heave their heads.

He passed by Masih as if Masih had suddenly become invisible. The boy's slippers flipped away; he kept running for his life. Masih looked up to see what the hell was going on. A flock of men and women were watching them from above.

The only thing missing now was them cheering, "Hercules, Hercules."

The boy got caught by one of the officers, who forced him to fall on his knees. His hands were cuffed, and similarly, each of them lying around were now being carried to the Rangers. Masih's jaw dropped, and when he averted his eyes, an officer stared at him in extensive shock.

"In my entire life, I've never seen anything like this...how could you? What are you, ten?

"What?" Masih squinted his eyes.

"Of course, you're high."

Chapter 26

Daydreamers

Half an hour later, Masih found himself inside a police station, sitting next to the boy. The rest were already taken to rehab, and their heads were shaved, shining under the sunlight as each left the police station.

"I knew it... I knew he was lying!" the boy muttered, shaking his head.

A man stepped out from the room across from them.

"Come in," said the man.

The boy nodded and went inside.

"Both of you," he added.

The boy smirked and looked at Masih, who still had no idea how he got there.

What if they found out about the box? About Sherin's shoes! About father buying me a TV? About me being the reason, my mother is going to die in a week? His eyes welled up.

"What are you waiting for? Come in, I said!" the man boomed.

Masih followed them.

The boy and Masih sat on the brown sofas by the wall, and across them sat a man in a black suit talking on his phone. There was a five minute of awkward silence. The man on the phone wasn't speaking. He kept listening to God knows what.

Finally, the clicking of the phone broke the silence.

"So, explain yourselves." He put his arms on the polished table, beside the globe which had Masih's attention.

The boy cleared his throat. "Jawad *jan*, how about I go first?" the boy said, looking at Masih.

Masih's head turned to the boy. Apparently, he was Jawad *jan*. He nodded and looked back at the globe, his mind going bonkers.

"You see, sir. We have a brother, our second brother. He's been lost for about three days now. Jawad... Jawad can't sleep at night since our brother has left the house." He gazed at Masih, and a tear fell from his eyes.

Masih turned his gaze to the globe, processing this tale.

"Our mother... she... she's in the hospital."

Masih's eyes glinted, and he looked at the man across from him. Their eye contact lasted for a few seconds, and the boy continued. "A friend suggested checking that area. We couldn't find him there too. We were just about to leave." He continued, "I mean... think about it, sir. Jawad and I are the only ones who are sober. Why else would we be there?" He added and looked at Masih, who nodded.

The man in the black suit nodded back and sighed. He signed two papers in a file in front of him. "You can go. But wait...what was your name again?"

Both cried, "Jawad."

The officer gazed at them strangely.

"Arvin, my name is Arvin," the boy said, rubbing his forehead.

They walked out of the room and the police station. Arvin firmly held Masih's hand. "Play along," he muttered, smiling at Masih.

After they turned to a street, the phoniness at last ended.

"Jawad?" Masih yelled, pulling his hand away.

"I saved your life! Do you want to spend your childhood in prison? Well, I don't mind, go on then and tell them the truth. That you were there for stolen money, which was itself stolen money!"

"It's for my mother," Masih cried, and his voice broke off.

The word mother welled up his eyes, brought lumps to his throat which were pounding aggressively, and his heart yearned for her warm long-lasting hugs, for her curses, for her kisses, Mother.

There was a pause, a woman carrying groceries passed by them as they were standing still in the narrow street.

"She makes you steal?" Arvin raised his eyebrow.

"No! She's going to die if I don't find the money. Thirty thousand in less than two weeks! A day already passed."

"Why didn't you take the money when you had the chance then?" Arvin said, lowering his gaze.

"Pity, you made me feel bad for you. Just look at yourself. I might be messy and stink as well, but at least I have control over myself."

Arvin smirked and shook his head.

"You got a point here, kid."

Arvin put his hand inside his pocket and pulled out black beads, mint gums, a scissor, and a couple of hundred notes and showed them to Masih.

"I'm sorry, I hope this makes up for it. I spent three hundred of your money. I was starving."

Masih glanced at his scraped hand outstretched and trembling. He took the money and left the rest.

Arvin threw them inside his bag. "I won't bother you again." Arvin turned and disappeared into the crowd.

~

Since he left home, the only thing he wished he could know somehow was the time. It had been a long time since dusk, so he figured it was ten or something when he arrived back near the bakery.

Masih threw himself on the ground and hit his head against the red building, which was the bakery. The rocks and the cold ground never felt so soft and comfortable. He couldn't feel his legs for a few minutes, and when he could, he wished he couldn't. His feet were throbbing.

He took off his shoes and had a glimpse of his swollen feet, but it didn't matter for now. He snatched the plastic and threw the earned money inside, wrapped it up, and tugged it inside his shirt.

~

Masih waited for the line to complete. This time no one gave him bread. However, instead of him, one man gave it to a mendicant woman with her little child asleep in her lap. Masih glared at her as she ate it and gave little pieces of it to the baby who just woke up. He averted his eyes, envying her existence.

I could've saved my money. Now I must change a hundred note.

He went to the shop next to the bakery and bought a biscuit which cost him ten Afghani. Masih went for the heaviest and largest packet at the same price. The shopkeeper said it was twenty Afghani for the one he chose.

With a frown on his face, Masih gave him the money. He couldn't stop looking at its empty packet after he enjoyed the best biscuits he had ever had, creamy yet tender and sweet.

"P-R-I-N-C-E..."

"So, you can read too, huh?" Masih twitched.

He turned to his left. Arvin propped against the red building sat next to him, cracking his knuckles.

Masih felt as if the colour drained from his face, and his lips trembled.

Arvin gazed at him strangely, then stood up and, just like that, disappeared.

It took him an hour to get back to his consciousness. Masih was still unaware of what he feared in Arvin. Was it the fact that he was robbed by him? Or arrested for the first time being eleven? Was it the way Arvin looked at him so innocently yet doing such an evil act?

Chapter 27

Innocent sins

The same gaze, the same words, the same humiliation...every door he knocked on, the owner kicked him out. Apparently, no shop wanted a burglar-looking boy to take care of the shop, and it was hard to find a place in a country where everyone else hunted each other's niche.

Another day down, Masih spent a hundred instead of getting anything. He lost money that day, and he earned not even a penny but was given a scar by one of the shopkeepers who owned a market of dry fruits. He threw a knife at him; he used to unwrap a carton of cookies. Masih kept insisting on just one bite. Instead, he received something else.

The scar was a deep, hued scar underneath his left eye, purple and scarlet. Under the starry night, there lay a galaxy in that scar, yet people were busy glancing at the headlights as he sat in their pathway. Perhaps some lives were just meant to be survived.

He chose the same place to stay that night, where he met that kind man. Maybe he'd show up again the next day, and in the hopes of tomorrow, he closed his eyes to sleep. But what to hope for when it was hope that scared you?

It's Ramadan, padar jan. You used to say Satan is chained, but then why I just met something today, something that Satan might fear too...I feel bad for Satan padar jan.

There are creatures ten times worse than him living happily.

His eyes slowly opened into a slit, then fully. The sky spun for a moment. Masih slid his hands over the hard ground to sit straight, and his hand crashed with something, a plastic pouch.

Masih looked around. People were in lines across the bakery. The plastic pouch lay right beside him as if it were his. He unhurriedly had a peek, a carton of those cookies he had been pleading for reclined right next to him. However, now, his longing self didn't crave them as much as he wanted them before, but he was pleased and couldn't stop smiling.

Masih pulled out the carton from the bag and opened it. Cream puffs, muffins, doughnuts, all kinds of cookies. He first began with the fluffy cream puffs, which melted in his mouth. He closed his eyes and permitted the sheer delicacy to sink in.

He folded the plastic bag, his eyes gleamed, looking at his leftover bakeries.

A baby cried hysterically. The same woman was sitting at the other end of the bakery, holding her baby. Without any hesitation, he carried the carton and approached her. "Here." He handed it to her.

The woman stared at him, awestricken.

"I know how you feel. Share it with your baby too."

"Not now. I'm fasting." The woman hid it under her green blanket.

Masih beamed at the baby boy whose eyes were adorned with *surma*. The baby giggled, scratching his nose and curling his toes.

"What a great day!" Masih shouted, looking at the open sky.

The man named Ayaar had been unconditionally kind, first a thousand Afghani then a carton of those cookies. But how did he know about the incident? That messed with Masih's mind.

Perhaps he was recording me from somewhere. Maybe that's why he laughed and pulled up his spiky hair gazing in that direction. Arvin is the bad guy.

When he mentioned his name under his tongue, Masih saw him coming towards him while carrying his bag. The bag and the way he came across didn't match at all.

Masih averted his gaze and recalled this didn't happen in the movies. It was not how it worked, so he pulled his shoulders back, puffed up his chest, and swaggered towards him. Arvin paused and glanced at Masih, strangely, coming closer.

"I think you don't know who I am?"

"What?" Arvin peeped around.

"So, you know too, huh?"

"What are you talking about?"

"I'm supposed to fight with you."

Arvin dropped his bag and wheezed until he couldn't inhale. Masih, however, was angry by standing there, looking at him, crying tears of laughter.

"Yes, yes laugh, for now. You will cry for it later."

"I think...I think there was something in those cookies." Arvin straightened his back, sniffing and striving not to laugh.

Masih had gone bonkers. "How do you know?"

"Did you check the bag?" Arvin chuckled.

Masih pulled out the plastic bag and had another glimpse. Three hundred Afghanis were lying inside it. He felt himself blushing again. It all made sense now.

"So... what was all this about?"

"Nothing..." Masih muttered, extremely disappointed.

"I'm really curious..." Arvin bit his chapped lips.

"Well, I thought we were in a movie scene. I had met a man before. You wouldn't get it..."

Arvin pursed his lips, nodded. His face turned scarlet. He burst into laughter all over.

After five more minutes, Arvin had to sit down somewhere or else he might have collapsed by all that staggering.

They walked to the school's pathway and sat down.

"I had not laughed this hard in the last three years of my life. God bless you, kid."

Masih hid his smile and remained quiet.

"So, you were the hero, huh?"

Masih gave him the stare.

"Okay, okay...so *bache film*. What's your name?"

"Jawad."

"Oh, come on. You still holding grudges about that?"

"Masih."

"Mmm, I had an uncle; his name was Masih..."

"Had?"

"Yeah, he spent his life thinking he was in a movie, ended up in the mental hospital..."

Masih stood up to leave. Arvin pulled him back down, giggling. "Okay, okay, I'm sorry. I'll stop now."

Masih sat down slowly and shook his head. He was the bigger guy dealing with a kid.

"So rich man, how much yet?"

"How much what?" Masih asked.

"Money, how much money could you save?"

"Oh, so that's why you're here. For my money?" Masih squealed.

"Of course! What else did you think?"

Masih gazed at him in contempt.

"Do you have a problem with sense of humour? Like a little happiness? Laughing?" Arvin asked.

There was a pause, Masih replied, "Nothing much, two thousand and something."

Arvin nodded slowly. "How much do you need?"

"Thirty..."

"Thirty... thirty what. Thousand?" Arvin gazed at him. His eyes widened.

Masih looked at him and sighed. "Yes."

"Then what the hell are you doing here?"

"What can I do?" Masih cried.

"How much time did you say?"

"Less than two weeks..."

For the next half hour, neither spoke a word. Their eyes were fixed on the songbirds over the orange fence and the grass behind it. They flew away and came back, then flew away again.

"My name will change into corpse, my corpse will turn into dust, my dust will merge with the wind, and you will breathe me one day..." Arvin recited in melancholy.

"So, it was because of a girl?" Masih glanced at him.

Arvin stared back in disappointment, saying, "I don't know why, they always say this about poets...anyway, do you want to save her life?"

"Of course, I want to."

"Then you have to do what I'll tell you, Masih."

"Never in a million years will I trust you."

"I'm not asking for your trust. You shouldn't trust me at all. If I don't get that which kills me every day, I will harm anyone. I can do anything."

"Then what's your point?"

"Stay away from me and leave me when in times I'll ask you."

"What's your plan?"

"Of course, it's a robbery!" He lowered his voice, peering.

"No. Are you crazy? That's not right," Masih boomed.

"Oh, really? What is right, Masih? What has been right all along? Your life? My life? Anyone has been right to you? Was that man right when he almost made you blind? Tell me?"

Masih gulped. He imagined the fork coming through again and again.

"Things don't just happen for us. You should know that by now."

"What if we got caught?" Masih howled.

"What can be worse than now?"

"At least we're alive..." Masih muttered.

"Death can't hurt as much as this does, now, can it? And you can't deny Masih, to rest is a luxury, and to live even in a luxury is labour."

"You mean you want to die?"

Arvin sighed, and Masih got his answer in that sigh of relief. Death for him a longing wish.

"What do you want me to do?" Masih asked.

"Thirty thousand is a lot of money. The chances of getting it in about a week are pretty rare, but we'll try our best," Arvin said.

"Why are you helping me? What are you getting from this?" Masih asked anxiously.

Arvin smirked. "You are a smart kid, but dumb too, occasionally."

"I'll just gain more experience, I guess," Arvin added.

Masih nodded, although deep down, he was certain that it was not just for the experience.

He's getting something out of it, but what?

Or maybe the reason for such kindness is that some get weary of tormenting themselves.

~

They were on the pathway, looking at the birds again since Arvin said they'd do something at night.

It was near dusk when Arvin stood up abruptly. "I'll be back," he said, not looking at Masih.

Masih's stomach growled. He clenched it and put his head on the ground. While glancing at the little rocks fallen over the pathway, his eyes shut down.

"Masih, Masih!" he felt hands gently moving him.

"Mmm." Masih opened his eyes and screamed, gaping at the masked face in front of him.

"Shush, it's me, Arvin."

Masih stood up and placed his hand over his heart.

"Is this the time to sleep?"

Masih looked up. The sky had never been this dull and gloomy. "What was I supposed to do then?"

"Here." Arvin handed him a packet of sponge cake, peach flavoured.

Masih finished it in seconds and gave the packet back to Arvin, who gave him a strange glance and threw it on the ground.

"What are you doing? I could've done that too." Masih picked it up and threw it inside the bag Arvin held up.

"You disgust me." Arvin shook his head.

Arvin pulled out another black mask, like the one he had covered his face with. He stepped closer towards Masih and bent down.

"What are you doing?" Masih whispered.

"Strangling you."

He wrapped the scarf around Masih's face, and the only thing uncovered were his eyes.

Arvin stood straight and took out the scissor from his pocket. "Keep this to yourself. Use only if needed." Arvin put it inside Masih's jean's left pocket.

Arvin pulled out a knife from his bag and slid it underneath the black bracelet he had on his right wrist. Masih looked at him as he rolled over his sleeve to hide the knife.

He glanced at Masih, whose eyes were fixed on the shape of the knife. "We won't harm anyone... right?" Masih asked.

"I don't know." Arvin heaved his bag and threw it over his shoulder.

"What do you mean I don't know?" Masih raised his voice.

Arvin stopped and turned to him. "Listen, I don't want to hear another word. Second, I don't enjoy stabbing people either, alright saint? If I have no other choice, that's what I'll do. Do you want your mother to live or not?"

"Where are we going?" Masih broke the first rule in less than a second.

Arvin gave him a dirty stare, and Masih kept his mouth shut for the sake of his life.

Masih peered around. The streets were empty except for a few stray dogs who were lying down across from them.

"They won't bother tonight." Arvin smirked.

About ten minutes along the way, Masih got the idea of where they were headed to, the same cookie shop. Arvin stopped across its door and observed the iron door with its gigantic lock. Arvin tilted his head and pulled out his knife. From his pocket, he took out a stretched bobby pin.

Masih stood third wheeling between Arvin and the door as Arvin was getting intimate with the lock. At the first few fragile clicks, Masih's heart virtually stopped, though now he was used to it. Another click and Arvin looked up at Masih, who stood beside him looking at the dark.

Arvin oiled the edge of the iron door with a piece of cloth and opened it carefully. He stepped inside, and Masih followed by. Masih's shoes were clicking on the cream and golden tiles inside, and Arvin's were slurping.

He showed Masih the palm of his hand, and Masih stopped right in the middle. He gestured his fingers first to his own eyes, then at the outside. Masih got his message and averted his gaze outdoors.

~

Arvin looked at the red light beaming. It was the security camera, but he couldn't care less. His face was unrecognisable anyway; however, he felt a chill in his spine when he remembered Masih if he did anything stupid...

Without looking anywhere else, Arvin went straight for the cashier. It was even more shocking for him to witness that the drawer was not locked at all. Arvin smiled, shaking his head. He secured the plastic bag covering his hand and opened the drawer.

It wasn't much, maybe a week or two's saving, but his face glowed. Arvin gradually emptied the drawer into his bag, returned it to its slot, and closed it. He stepped out from there, took two biscuits filled with cherry jam, and gestured to Masih to leave. They walked out of the shop, munching on the biscuits as they left the area.

They found a quiet spot somewhere in *Karte Seh*.

"You seemed like a complete professional," said Masih.

"I'll take that as a compliment." Arvin began cracking his knuckles as they lay on the grass

"We aren't going back there, okay?"

Masih nodded.

"This time, we better do something bigger. A cookie shop won't do."

"Five thousand Afghani is a lot," Masih cried, and his voice broke off.

"But it's not enough. It's not thirty now, is it?"

"I've never been in this area that much. I don't know about here," Masih said, looking at the tall building outside the park. It had statues of peacocks on its rooftop.

"Because it's for the wealthy, for those brats."

"Then how come you knew every street so well?" Masih asked.

"I don't like being asked questions. Keep that smart mouth closed."

"Why are you treating me like a kid?"

"I don't know...let me think, maybe because you are."

"A kid doesn't go through what I have. A kid doesn't see what I've witnessed."

"A kid in Afghanistan does."

Chapter 28

A young boy's diary

"Is it the peacock house?"

"What?" Arvin asked, wrapping his head with his black scarf.

"The house we're...you know, getting in tonight."

"First of all, there is no we. I'm going on my own—"

"What? No, I'm coming too," Masih cut him off.

"There is no use for you to come. And no, it's not the peacock house." Arvin threw his bag down. "Take care of my bag until I'm back. Don't you dare touch it. We clear?"

"I'm hungry," Masih muttered.

"I'll bring you something along the way."

"Not cookies again."

"It's midnight, for God's sake!"

He vanished after leaping over the red fences inside the park. Masih turned his back on the building with peacocks and propped his head against a pine tree.

Masih opened and closed his fists under the moonlight to feel it thoroughly. He shrugged a little as the chilly wind rustled the leaves. The night felt peaceful and opaque except for the slight white light he collected from the full moon.

A howl twitched him a bit and urged him to turn. It came from a remote area, and he made sure by observing the fences that there was no chance for one hungry wolf to go inside the park.

His eyes stopped on the bag.

It's hefty since Arvin lifts it from one shoulder to the other constantly along the way. It's large so whatever is inside isn't just one thing. It's important since Arvin keeps it close to his chest, even when he sleeps. It's daunting because I am told not to even look at it, let alone to open it.

Masih averted his eyes and stood up. He fooled around for a few minutes, clasped his hands, swung around the tree as he held on to it, and let his right hand loose. He looked up at the pines, each swinging along with the rhythm of the wind, like a baby looking up at the dangles of his cradle.

He closed his eyes and inhaled the scent of the pines, then curved his lips upwards. It smelled like the oil his mother used to put on her thick curly hair, the oil his father gifted her on their anniversary.

One pinecone hit the ground. Masih picked it immediately and threw it in the air, then caught it as it fell. Minutes later, he discarded the pine since now this, too, bored him.

To touch or not to touch. Suddenly that bag was the most alluring, to have a peak was the most tempted he felt in a while. Doing something he was told not to do for his safety was rare, something he wasn't asked to do, but wanted to do it desperately.

Its skin was rough, just like its owner's, stiff and detached. Would it overflow with something like the snow? Or packets of cancer-inducing? Or hued lighters? He put his hand over his heart for a second and took a deep breath.

The sound of the zip opening was loud enough to wake up the world in the dead of night. It was dark inside it, a universe left to be explored. Masih shoved his shaking hands slowly inside as if something will jump and bite his fingers.

He found soft clothes, loose beads, a packet of gum, and something hardback. He made sure to touch every single corner, every spot, and feel it all.

Is it a box? Is there a gun inside it?

Masih pulled it out without thinking twice. It fell from

his hands as he started laughing. He smacked his head and chuckled, still not sure if it was what he saw.

He drew his fingers and tapped over the book's brown hardback cover with the tip of his nails. He opened it right away and had a fast peek till the end just to see, the dense papers were filled with handwritten words in black ink.

The handwriting was so alluring, it compelled him to do it again. Illustrations were drawn from page to page, a flower, a girl's eyes, and thick brows, a headless silhouette, cells, a ring, but there was no sign of him in these pages, nothing that could assure that there was a possibility of this being Arvin's.

Masih jumped back to the first page and read the poem...

Don't watch my face, stare at my heart.
Don't count my age, I'm older than the stars.
Learn from the evils, but don't get possessed.
Don't judge my fate, it's a complicated work of art.
Don't pity my mistakes, nor enjoy my success.
Lessen the hate and then just be, who you are.

Thunder, irregular roars, purple flickers. They closed the windows, letting out a nervous snicker. I smiled, inhaling the scent of damp earth, music to my ears...

It's a beautiful day today...the sky is gloomy, it's pouring rain and mother is making *bolani* for me and my cousins who are playing FIFA, Father is out of town again. I feel bad for not missing him...I wish there were a way to know him all over again, a different approach.

I feel strange looking at my ring, I love her, but there is a feeling of doubt, not about her but me. I doubt this ring, I don't trust it since I saw it in the market but nodded when they liked it. It's always been about them, even if I want to, it's still about them. They say love is blind, but I highly doubt it. Love is not blind, it's just procrastinating what you see until it reaches a point when both break each other's heart so it's better if they say it in the first place, but I'm a hypocrite and I can't help it.

What would happen if I said no... not just the ring but... what if I said this is not the life I want? The truth is, I don't even know the life that I want, all I know is I'm still feeling nothing but estrangement. There's a thing about those melancholic romantic songs... those movies, art, maybe they messed up with my mind. She doesn't feel like the one, even though I tried for her to be, she's just like those flocks of loud people, nothing like me and it's a good thing, I wouldn't wish it upon my worst enemy, I know how it feels to be this way, a stranger to everything that exists... I'm foreign to love, but maybe you know it's love when for the first time in the presence of someone, you feel like you're alone just like you would after finally escaping the gathering you never wanted to be a part of, and you lay down on the cold side of the pillow, and they are there right beside you... I want that, I crave that.

~

I can't believe the wedding day is already fixed, on the eighth of October, eight days later...it's funny how I'm starting this new journey with a new journal, I like this one, it's fancier. Sara gifted me this, my fiancé...I blush when I think of her, well I blush every five seconds, but it's severe when it's about her, even the first letter of her name drowses me...but she doesn't know.

I fear to feel cold in a warm expected hug, I fear to feel hated in what they call love, I fear regretting all my life, believing in the wrong one...

~

We went to the restaurant, the one her sister who came with us (third wheeling) chose, I was too shy to say anything, and I think Sara had already told her sister what to say. I caught her raising her eyebrows and gesturing at her younger sister, but I pretended I haven't noticed, she tries to be someone she's not

166

around me. I don't like her when she's not being herself when she's copying my timidness while that's not even who I am. I want her to be herself so I could be me. I felt like a hypocrite ordering the same thing she did while I didn't want pizza, I wanted meatballs, I didn't want coke, I wanted Fanta, but chose that black liquor to look cooler. So, I know the moral behind this is that now days simply just being yourself is terrifying. You must be likeable and please everyone, act as they want, say only what they want to hear and live your life according to social standards... This fear of being yourself will go away with time, but the fake personality won't so please, be you. Who am I talking to?

You see people
I see monsters
You see crowds
I see a flock of dragons
I a tiny rabbit
Any second attacked
I wish to vanish just like that
You walk on the pathway
I seek the corners
You have relations
And I have attachments
I a pleasing puppet
Their expressions command
You ask questions
But I assume answers
You hear compliments
And I seek an escape from them
Big eyes surround me then
Each consumes me as I thaw
You witness arguments
I become each, warfare in my head
Conflicts are my dead-end

You fear loneliness
I live my sanctuary and a loyal friend
Find a way and shed my skin
Let me step out from myself

~

Mother's never been this happy before. The last time I saw her dancing was at her brother's wedding four years back, she used to be happier back then... She looked up, pursed her lips, her hands were on her hips as she twisted and turned and circled then laughed, she laughed at me as I smiled at her folding my white t-shirt she bought from the tailor. She took my hand and heaved me, and I danced with her swinging my long arms and legs, clumsy, silly, we snorted, and we danced. What a day...

~

I can't sleep again, it's two am, even the crazy neighbour turned off the light's and fell asleep, but I haven't...

~

Four am... where do I begin? It has been more than an hour that the neighbour's phone next to my room is ringing, it's four in the morning. The ringtone is Nokia, I couldn't sleep tonight, so I watched a movie and I stayed up to pray *Fajr* then sleep, but this ringtone is strange to me, and I don't know...it feels like...I can't help but wonder, how is that person not giving up calling? That person might know, it's four in the morning, he's been calling since three or two am nonstop. The caller has not lost hope, that person has the phone on hand and is calling, and calling, and calling and he keeps listening to the same beeping voices, and the voice at the end which says very politely with her gushed voice, "The person you're trying to reach is busy, please try again later." he doesn't try later, he tries right away all over again and again and again and then some give up after not even letting the first call last till the end, they end it in five seconds. How different, how two different mind-sets, two different hopes, one hopeful and then hopeless... It's time I should sleep rather than writing paragraphs about the calls regarding my neighbour lol, good night, myself.

~

He came back, today... The plates were thrown down from the table, a glass was flung at me which I miraculously dodged, I guess God just wants me to live, never asks if I want to live like this or maybe I should start telling him more, I'll start telling God what I want. Mother once again wiped the floor with clothes, the shattered glass cut her finger and she was bleeding. I finished my food as if he weren't screaming drunk from the hall, as if mother weren't sobbing looking down as if I had a sense of what I was swallowing, but I ate till the end. I'm tired.

~

The worst feeling in the world, the voice you once loved scares you, the people you thought loved, hate you...sometimes I'm at the edge of vulnerability that even a certain look can push me away, and sometimes here I am beaten up and still smiling like a dork as I write. My nose was bleeding and, his fists are heavy, but I'm glad I could save her this time. She ran away to our neighbour's, and I ran to my room, we all are running, from what exactly I don't know, we're just running. Maybe tonight no matter how much I try, I can only be sad and that's alright.

~

I was so high, the highest place I have ever been to. It was so beautiful, but at the same time terrifying. Some houses looked so little from where I was standing. Their rooftops were the colour pink, a place I had never seen, nor been in. On the other side was a hill, on top of it a huge black Eagle, which I scared away, I screamed at it. Looking down was breath-taking, I was levitating, feeling the wind, but finally, I managed to come down, it was the most different dream I ever had...

~

"I haven't seen a writer who ate dinner and went to sleep. He wants to become a writer..." Father smirked and snorted, saying this as he high-fived with my father-in-law on the dining table. Sara also laughed, everyone laughed, I did, too, and it wasn't fake at all, but I was laughing at how much one can be hated, humiliated, I was laughing at how strange this all was, me sitting there, it's the week of my wedding day, my about to be wife doesn't even know me although we've been together for a year now.

She doesn't laugh at my jokes like this, the only time I can make her laugh is when I'm trying to explain myself when I talk about life, then is when she laughs the most... And as I write oh, like the insane I'm laughing cause when it stops is when I began to weep.

They looked at me and asked me, looking at my face, "Why are you so quiet? Don't you have anything to say?" I just smiled and let him answer for me like always and he came up with another one of his amazing jokes, I'm always the subject of the funniest ones...she laughed again though, even harder. Sometimes it's not what they say, but the way they say it and I wish I couldn't pick that up. I have words about the stars, the moon, life, death, freedom, nostalgia, my dreams, my feelings but not for them, for the ones who are worth telling to. I'm the most talkative ranting person to myself, to my diary and perhaps someone, someday...

Alone
And away
Wish I could get in their heads
To make them forget
From the letters of my name
To whatever I've said

From the way I've made them feel
To the strange ways, I'm perceived
I'll be that suppressed word which was never spoken
A forgotten dream from which one was sometime awoken
Not caring, nor striving
Feelings dying
No more trying
To mend a heart whining
Away
And alone
Wish I was a memory, bypassed to be remembered
To the murmur of the winds, I'll order
Through them, will speak to them each
The coastline will be our border
I the crashing wave, they cannot reach
To the sand simmered by the sun under their feet
I'll confide to be my warm distant hugs
From a falling star, they'll ask of me
Will reply, it does not know of such
Breathed in a way, not existing at all, wild tender
To the exotic, I want to be surrendered
Alone and away
Lonesome flying
Careless crying
Hitting rock bottoms
I want to be forgotten

~

I try to smile and say I don't care, then turn around on the other side of my bed leaving it damp from the tears I confess. I don't care for my unimportant dreams that I thought would happen one day, I don't care that she doesn't love me and I know it, I don't care that I'm falling out of love too, I don't care to the point I care too much... people's emotion controls me, maybe they'd understand and maybe I can explain it too, but I can't make it... and I'm not letting them in, since I'm fighting for my own space. And I might be searching for withdrawals, but I wish they don't let me be alone, then I think of escapes from myself.

I've guarded myself, badly.

I saw my name bleeding on the paper because of all the words they said and here I am, terrified of being the reason for someone's tears...

It comes in tides and I don't even try to stay afloat, yet I'm not drowning today, I see the big ones as a getaway. Shores are the witness, simmered sand doesn't like cold feet leaving imprints just to run away, ruined pretty castles so they won't want me to stay, hurt enough and gave rise to vicious waves. Seas want me out, gravels clearing my signs, while I just want to evaporate...

~

10pm, I was peacefully reading "Body language for dummies" for reasons I'm afraid to even write down. I was enjoying myself as we didn't have electricity, but it didn't last...just heard a loud voice of explosion, it brought the wave of the wind which carried thousands of bad news with it, went further to inform what it had witnessed, the house shook a little, but I can't calm my heart. I have my phone on my hand, turned on its torchlight, I don't think my heart is healthy anymore, it has been tortured mercilessly. The thing is that, now, living in Afghanistan isn't sad anymore, it's funny. And the moments I'm waiting for makes me laugh sometimes.

We're too young to be this hopeless. We're too old to run away again. Over the mountains. Cross the seven seas, just to be called immigrants, who can't find a place in this world. We're too innocent, to be punished so severely. What is our fault? Kindly let me know.

As I'm writing, people are dying, I imagine the face of the mother informed of her son's demise as he was on a bus on his way home. The child watching faces looking at him strangely, he doesn't know his father is in the room next to him, not ever opening his eyes. I'm tired, these two words are probably the words I've used the most in this frantic diary, I think they are on every page. You know... I can't help but wonder if my death will be by one of these, by one of these explosions, a missile or maybe a gunshot... I can't help but think what it will be like if one of them hits this window right across from me if one blew up near our home. Then it would be over because I see no other end.

One hundred people they said, the man on the TV.... he said it in a way as if he wasn't talking about humans, as if it wasn't the calculation of dying humans, as if they were some groceries, something, useless. Getting a sense that it is like that, it's starting to become like that more often, not just physically, but mentally we are no longer valued, feelings are the last thing one can care about. They're too busy thinking about their empty stomachs, there's a war in every house, we're too exhausted to fight the enemies when it's a war within ourselves. Here's to the day this country will start to breathe again... but for now, there's so much to cry for, but no endurance to do so.

Kills me slowly
Kills me slowly
Every breath
And I want to be breathless

Take my years
Let them be yours
For all I've lived
Are seconds of fear and phoney hopes
Guns and missiles
Dangle from my cradle
Mourning families

Sing me to sleep
Have my eyes
There's no strength left to weep
Take my eyes
Let them be yours
For all I see
Is that pretty girl
Her head lied over a notebook
Her blood is going cold
Her father waiting for her at home
Muttering, she's alright
But she has already died
Take my ears
Let them be yours
For all I listen
Are the wails of that mother
Cursing the earth
For consuming her twenty-five-year-old son
And I want to be breathless

I try to write happy words, but they seem to run out so quickly. And when you wake up to missiles…something dies in you, perhaps the will to live, or to do anything. You just want to sit and stare. I'm tired of feeling like I'm a heavyweight on someone's shoulder, I'm tired of feeling threatened the moment I leave the house, I'm tired of smiling at the moments when they say those words which make me sob later when I'm alone, I'm tired of coming to the point where I'm starting to believe things are going to get worse but never better because that's what is happening, I'm tired of feeling tired... I was craving my diary to write this and just wanted to come back home as soon as I could, I'm tired of being sad on the days I should be happy because of those who can't see me happy, I'm tired of the toxic people who I meet years later but they are still the same and every single time their words get sharper and louder to the point, I just make an awkward smile because I don't know what to do. After all, I came to the point I just lost myself. I just pray to Allah to not be in this state till the next Eid. I want to be free from this prison I'm tired of having to experience that scary gaze of them which lasts for eternity, I'm tired of keeping my head down and feeling embarrassed in front of my mother when I'm being harassed by brainless jokes he pokes at my face and I know that she notices too, I'm tired of thinking with myself if these things happened before too but I didn't notice or maybe I'm now sensitive, I'm tired of trying to change myself to not be the way I am...

~

The hall was massive! I can't believe it's happening tomorrow. The two chairs were on the stage, which were being decorated with pearls. It was more like my throne than a chair. I can't wait to sit there with Sara. Father said he has a surprise for me, he's been acting kinder lately and used a limited amount of curse words, plus it's for the first time in my life that I haven't seen him smoking for two days long.

Mother can't stop smiling, her friends came today and saw the bedroom mother has been busy decorating these past few days. They said it's like a king's bedroom, we have lots of money, he has, it's not mine, I haven't earned a penny.

~

She laughed at that forehead when it was raised saying, "it looks like stairs" little did she know, it was the stairs which made her climb all the way up, all this way... My fiancé, Sara chuckled looking at her mother's failed attempts on finding the right texture of foundation to cover up. Her mother averted her eyes embarrassed; I could feel the warmth of her rosy cheeks standing ten feet away, her heartbeat was synching with mine. I'm anxious all the time but she was this time too. I saw her slowly wipe her face while her daughter, my fiancé was talking to me, but I was hearing and I wasn't seeing I was watching a woman breakdown, another woman apart from my mother.

What does that even mean? Why would you cover up? It's something that deserves to be shown off to the world to see how many battles you've fought, each line is a defeated war, a lap of your marathon, embrace them wrinkles, they're deep and loyal, unlike almost everything...

~

Sometimes I just want to close my eyes, crumple, and jump in a never-ending, deep dark hole...

The crazy neighbours are up again. It's Friday night and I'm listening to the laugh and joy and the singing, the funny words they say inside my pitch-black room, I decided to turn down my music to hear their laughs. One of them has a contagious one, made me laugh too, a little girl snorts every five minutes, then there are the boys who want a world war when they lose in, God knows whatever they are playing, I think they're playing cards. Five seconds later and here comes the angry mother with another woman who's probably the guest tonight, I think they are sisters, they sound familiar.

The women daunt them, but there's a sweetness in the one of their curses as if they love seeing what they are seeing in that small room of kids gathered head-to-head having the times of their lives and if only someone could tell them live this moment, it won't come again, cherish it and you're so lucky to be having fun in this bleak world. I feel so lonely.

~

It's weird how sometimes the ones who are meant to be the most trusted and the closest, can be like a stranger to you. Can't tell them what you did, what you want, how you feel, I don't even know what the purpose of them is anymore. It feels like having strangers in your life with whom you can never share your happiness, nor your tears, the ones to whom you're afraid to say your dreams because it feels like even though they don't know what it is, but they already hate it and the only thing your heart keeps telling you is to keep quiet and carry on.

It's again one of those nights I feel a universe is inside me flourishing feelings out of this world. They flow slowly but is intense like a force, again makes me write what I can't understand, but only feel, the music gives life to this universe by every beat, a flow of colours spread in me, they colour a dark space, it's beautiful and only I can see

Collapsed, collapsed, we collapsed...

~

I'm feeling something I can't describe, is it my fault to not have the words? But I'll just write it, not how it shouldn't be or make sense, but how I feel it. It's past midnight the dogs are barking and I'm hearing the wind blowing outside, it's time to sleep everyone said except for me, just staring at the wall and sang a pretty song which just came in my mind, and I named it "butterflies" inspired by the painting on the wall above my bed. I wonder if I'd ever get the courage to sing it in front of someone. I should sleep but my mind wants to think so I'm sitting on my bed thinking what is life. It's so weird people across the world so far from me living lives so differently... What is everyone in this second going through? Maybe someone's happiest moment and someone just lost everything he loved, or someone like me feeling like this which doesn't have a word, but I'll name it, I would like to call it "1 am thoughts" so if there is anyone else going through it would understand and I, too can use it when I know exactly what it is.

~

A sudden fear is making my heart go crazy, it's making me weak, it's again one of those thoughts, those kinds which keep me awake at nights, which slowly fades me and makes me lose another piece of joy which was left, the thought of what if I never made it out, out of this, this thing that I'm caught up in, don't even want to call it my life, it has never been mine. I feel disgusted with myself, the way I'm whining, complaining to a journal of how I never took any responsibility and let them do whatever they wanted just for a second of peace. My life is ruined and nor did I find any truce, what is the whole point of this? Why am I living?

~

At this time tomorrow I'll be sitting on that chair, she will be beside me, I'll be faking laughs, I hope she would see that and ask me once and then I could tell her how much I feel for her, but half of what I feel is she feels nothing at all, that I'd rather be somewhere far away from all of this crowd alone with her, together with our vacancy, and just listen to the ocean crashing, on top of a hill, watching the city lights, the cars passing and whooshing, the chilly breeze would make her shiver and I'll take off my jacket for her. She would rest her head upon my shoulder, we will talk about life, I want that to be my wedding night.

~

My father is in his car, I can listen to the song he's playing it's Farhad Darya's, *"sanama hey sanama"* We're just leaving for the hotel, yes, it's my wedding day, as I'm standing near my room's doorway, writing on my journal, I can see my room clean and shimmering, but only I can see the hollowness. I've spent myself here, alone, the thing that terrifies me is spending it alone but with someone. He's calling me, we're having a ride like father and son, I'm happy...

~

The next page was empty. Just when Masih embarked on turning it once more, rapid footsteps approached him. He closed the book and tossed it inside the bag, put it exactly as it was, and jumped to his feet when his name was called.

"What are you doing?" Arvin asked him, looking at his

trembling lips.

Masih choked on words as he opened his mouth to answer.
"You alright?" Arvin added.

Masih nodded.

"Anyway..." Arvin unleashed a bundle of five hundred note cash from his pockets. He pulled up the bag, laying right beside Masih, who was still shaking. Arvin turned his face around and rummaged inside his bag. For a second, he paused. Masih's heart ached. Arvin turned and threw his bag on the ground. Arvin sighed as he leaned on the tree.

"Oh, you were hungry?" Arvin asked, searching his pockets. He pressed his lips together and pulled out a packet of peanuts wrapped in a plastic pouch. He handed it to Masih. The touch of Masih's cold hands urged Arvin to withdraw his hand.

"Damn! You're cold. No wonder you look like you've been stealing something instead of me." Arvin grinned. "Here." Arvin took off his leather jacket, Masih grabbed it.

Arvin sat across from him, cracking his knuckles. "So, aren't you going to ask me anything?"

Masih stared at him, wearing down the salty peanuts.

"God... I'm taking you to a doctor tomorrow, but I think it's going to be a phycologist or something since you've lost your mind, it doesn't matter what I tell you. So, it was crazy, kid! I thought they were smarter than this. The camera was down. They were using a lock! Are you kidding me? I can break those locks with a bobby pin: seven thousand, my friend. But I ain't spending a penny on you. You're better off brainless. It's for mother *jan*, I mean your mother, *jan*."

"Where's your mother?" Masih spoke at last.

After a lengthy pause, Arvin said, "So you're alright? Anyway, good night kid, it's been a long day." Arvin laid straight on the grass and turned his back to Masih, doing what he was best at, keeping it all to himself. Still, said a few words before falling asleep and after being aesthete that he was, "You know, kid? I wonder how it would be if we forgot life for a moment and not lived life, but lived us, our own existence..."

Masih tucked his hands under Arvin's jacket and stopped shivering. He looked at the full moon, doing what he was best at, daydreaming.

The moments I'm waiting for makes me laugh sometimes...

Chapter 29

You're a mystery to me

"Where next?" Masih moaned, his mouth stuffed with hot and spicy shawarma.

"You just keep walking with me." Arvin coughed in his hands and rubbed them together.

"Where is your family?" Masih kept his gaze on his meal.

"Dead." Arvin glanced at him.

Both caught the drowsy red eyes peeking from the corner of the street. Masih looked up at Arvin.

"You stay here for a second." Arvin halted Masih, looking at the man, and left towards him. Arvin nudged the man inside the narrow street and the view blocked for Masih.

He shrugged and kept munching on his steaming hot shawarma, which tasted delicious and tender.

"I had seen him at the bridge. He was lying there. What did he want?" Masih asked when Arvin came back.

"Nothing. You mind your own business; this has nothing to do with you."

"This is why we came all the way? From one park to another?" Masih whined.

"Oh, well, I'm sorry, I don't own a five-star hotel. So terribly sorry for this inconvenience, Mr Masih!"

"What's the point of coming here? That park was better than park *Shahr-e now* and had such a good view..."

"Could you just shut up for a second?" Arvin said out loud, looking around the green area.

Families were gathered around the park. They glanced at Masih and Arvin, they looked to be getting uncomfortable by the boys' presence.

"Come." Arvin beckoned Masih.

"Where now?"

"At the other spot. Somewhere at the ends."

"But why?"

Arvin turned.

"I SAID WHY?" Masih repeated screaming.

"Because people don't like addicts around them!" Arvin cried and looked at Masih at last.

It was obvious for Masih, still, from somewhere deep within, he liked to believe what he had in mind from the moment they met — Arvin was a superhero disguised as the villain. Like he had seen Snape in Harry Potter, though Arvin ruined it for him, the idea of him being the good guy. How could an addict be a good guy?

The only living things unbothered by their existence were the songbirds and insects at the corner, near the ruddy fences.

"What are you going to do with me?" Masih spoke after an hour of silence.

"What do you mean?"

"You know what I mean."

"No, I don't know what the hell you mean! You're the strangest kid I've seen in my life!"

"There were others before me?"

"God..." Arvin sank his face in his hands.

"Listen, if I wanted to kidnap you or whatever the hell you think I am doing, I wouldn't have waited this long and bear your annoying little... okay?

"You're an addict..."

"Well, surprise, surprise then!" Arvin stood up, cursing, and left the area.

He left his bag lying on the grass. Masih waited for five minutes before he fetched it. He rummaged in the sack for the book and pulled it out. He went to the page where he had stopped reading earlier and turned the sheet, but it was empty.

He looked back after a shadow fell across from him, and thankfully it was a stray cat. Masih exhaled. His heart about to stop beating.

He turned the pages till the end only to see deserted pages. He closed it and threw it back inside the bag.

What about the little one? He ran for the bag.

"Masih!"

Masih threw himself on the ground, right beside the bag. "I was about to capture a spider! It was just like the movie Spiderman! What do you want?" Masih covered himself with the first thing that popped up. It always had to be about a movie.

"Aren't you hungry?"

"I am," Masih replied.

"Then come on. I have half an hour before I leave."

"To where?"

"I can't tell you. Once we're done eating. You'll come back and stay here, alright?"

"Yes. I mean, I will, alright, whatever...someone has to guard that bag, anyway..."

"No, no, I'm taking the bag with me."

"But why?" Masih cried.

"What's wrong with you? Honestly, I'm getting worried for you. Anyway, come, it's getting late."

The last time Masih had been in a restaurant was on his tenth birthday. Just him, his father, and mother. His parents ordered burgers, the cheap ones, and asked for kebab for Masih. Lied, they didn't feel like having kebabs, and the burger was better for them. Lied that the coke was too fizzy so he could have more. Lied about everything to give him everything they could never have.

Masih swallowed his tears with every bite he took. He was getting even better at pretending...

Arvin tossed a tissue at him to wipe his mouth once he

finished.

Something about Arvin's presence would make it easier, so he didn't hesitate and spoke his mind. "What if she died? What if my mother couldn't make it, like my father?"

"Do you love them?"

"What kind of question is this?" Masih asked in irritation.

"Yes, or no?"

"Yes," Masih replied.

"Then they'll never die."

"But how can I ever talk to them? Or see them?" Masih asked hopelessly.

"When in love, you'll be talking quite often out loud, but not with that person, but with them living in your head, heart, and in front of your eyes. Sometimes you don't even get to see them, but they are there, always."

Masih couldn't help but smile and said, "I don't want to lose her."

"If something is remembered, how can it be lost?"

Masih beamed.

"Alright now. You go and stay at that spot until I'm back."

"When will you come back?" Masih asked him.

"If I didn't till tomorrow, live like this never happened, and we never met."

"What's going on?"

"Did you hear me?"

Masih nodded.

Arvin sighed and left the table.

~

Why is it always me? Why am I not bearable? Why every time... they must leave? How many times? I will stand up but to have to do it again ruins the idea of ever standing if it's just another fall...

Masih got lost in his thoughts, ambling on the streets the next morning after spending the night alone at that spot in the park. His thoughts were being interrupted by the growling of his starving stomach. Not even a penny he had. Arvin was the one who retained all the money.

Masih smirked at his own idiocy. At least he acquired fifteen hundred, and if he couldn't save his mother, for which he had only two days left, at least he could eat for some time, enough stamina to mourn her.

His legs were twitching. He sat on the pathway, gazed at the ground, and raised his hands, back to where it all began.

Masih shoved his head between his skinny thighs, bearing the ache in his famished stomach.

Sometimes broken things mend by force more powerful than the cause of their wreckage, and sometimes that was what happened to broken hearts.

His hand, pulled down by a weight. He looked up, a wad of money, not the ordinary ones, but those greens. The ones for which he once begged his father to buy for him, its fake ones, of course. And now it was there, real and a lot of them.

"Boo!" Arvin popped up in front of his face and sat beside him, chuckling, and cracking his knuckles.

"I'm hungry," Masih said, giving him the money.

"Oh, come on. When are you not?"

Arvin beckoned the young boy selling gums across from the street. The boy ran towards them.

"Take this hundred Afghani and bring a burger. Keep the change." Arvin winked, looking at Masih.

"Keep the change? You robbed a bank or something?" Masih said, clenching his stomach.

"Something like that. It's a hundred dollars in total."

"I thought you left me."

"For a moment, I did too." Arvin scratched the tip of his nose. His nails cracked and burned.

"I can see what you've been up to." Masih looked away aggrieved.

"Arvin clenched his fist and hid his hands under his coat.

"I'm sick Masih, I'm terribly sick."
"Then get well!" Masih's eyes teared up.
"Some things aren't that easy."
"You think this is easy?"
"I die every day." Arvin sighed.
"Then don't."
"To live what?"
"To live what I'm living. Do you think it's easy for me? Should I go and get high, too, then? My mother is about to die. My father died months ago. I'm homeless, living with an addict, and I'm a dumb kid with all the excuses. Tell me, should I get wasted then?"

Arvin huffed and turned his back to Masih.

I just want to help, but you just want to hurt. Masih thought.

The kid arrived with the burger. Masih took the biggest bite the second he had it and finished it promptly.

"You don't tell me where we go, you don't tell me where this money comes from, and yet you expect me to not get mad..." Masih mumbled, ambling with Arvin.

The Mullah *sahib* called the *Maghreb* adhan, and Arvin rushed inside a store. He got out of the store with a water bottle and dates.

"Oh, so you fast? Impressive."
"Shut up..." Arvin prompted him.

Masih chuckled, and just then, that same man was staring at them, lurking under the shadowed wall.

"Is he your friend?" Masih asked.

"I hope so, but people like me don't have friends." Arvin left towards the man, and they were out of his sight. After a minute, Arvin came back, jogging to him.

"You're not going to tell me, are you?" Masih implored.

"Nope."

Masih caught Arvin muttering and looking to his side several times along the way.

Is this the love he was talking about?

They stopped near the door of a small house. Arvin knocked, and it opened to them shortly. A slender man with missing front teeth opened the door, peeked around and permitted them to enter.

"You go inside and stay there. Lock the door and don't open. We have keys ourselves. Don't open the door, got me?" Arvin gave Masih orders.

"You're leaving me alone in here?"

"It's better than those parks where starving dogs wander around, don't you think?"

"You're going robbing with that enormous bag of yours?" Masih asked.

"What's you and your obsession with this worn-out bag of mine?

"No, no, the kid's got a point," the man spoke for the first time. "It's not easy to run with that," he added.

Masih was really liking this *kaka*.

Arvin pulled it off his shoulder and handed it to Masih. "You touch one thing, and I'll kill you."

"Yeah, yeah, like I love to touch your dirty stuff to get myself sick," Masih grunted.

"I'm just warning you. I get signals from it whenever someone else opens it just so you know."

Arvin and the man left, and Masih locked the door. He ran back into the empty room, took off his shoes, and felt the hard red carpet. A thermos, a cup, and a few chocolate bars were lying in the corner. He wished there was a TV. It's been ages since he saw one, yet he had to do something more important than that. For a second, he did get sceptical if Arvin really meant what he said but couldn't care less. He suspected Arvin was just a softy, pretending to be the bad guy.

Masih threw the bag and opened it right away. He shoved his hands inside it and pulled out the little notebook.

He opened it softly, saying, *Bismillah*.

Chapter 30

A young boy's catastrophe

I'll set my soul free
Even when I'm trapped
Oh, I'll sing inside my cell
All the happy songs, that I've never had
There will be a window
A ray of light will find its way in rad
The shadow of the bars will fall beautifully on the floor
All I see is art, in my pain, in this place
In my broken laughs
The way the walls will crumble
Will make it up for the paint
The songbirds will sing
And I will carve their words, yet again
I've set my soul free, even if I'm trapped...

The funny thing is that nothing compares to the pain I've endured being away from writing, not even all this misery, not even these prison bars, not even these crippling walls, nor my mother's tears I saw today. I saw her face after ten days, ten days and she was unrecognisable, ten days and we died. Yet nothing can be compared to the pain of having something to write, but having nothing to write on, having so much to write for. It's so dour, my writing has feelings, and I can't feel anything anymore. They don't like me in here, they don't like anything I do, from the way I breathe to the way I move, to the way I talk. Maybe because I don't talk, at all. I haven't spoken a word, and it's been ten days. Are they worried for me? Or I'm just annoying them. I like it, I'm enjoying, I'm dying.

~

As a kid, I used to hate nights because then I had to sleep. Isn't that crazy? Now when it's night and I think of tomorrow, I drown in a wave and hope that I won't wake up. I want to sleep, and I want to do that forever. Dying is a relief after living every second in the fear of death...

~

Seconds passed together with me, they were mine, but I couldn't notice, now that I know how many gems I've lost, it's too late to think about how precious they were and how I should've spent them. The younger those gems were the more value they held, the value of my childhood are immersed in those gems from the days I ruled my world, cared about nothing, no one could stop me, and I was genuinely happy. My heart pounded faster not because of anxiety, anger, hopelessness, or helplessness, but only because my little heart needed rest to take all that joy. I would forget a nightmare not by forcing myself to sleep again, but by remembering a wonderful dream which wasn't rare like nowadays. I lost my gems through time, I was happy to give them all, I was fooled by the image I had of growing. I would've done anything to let those seconds pass quickly, but now I would do anything to take them back...sometimes "If I died..." isn't an assumption, sometimes it's all one wants...

~

Fifteen days, still the same month...what can I do but only hope? I can't ask for what I'm constantly thinking about, I can't ask that for you, I can't ask anything for you from him who is the Almighty Allah, the most merciful. I'm talking to you mother as if you're the one who will read this doomed note, another page of my frantic diary, but someday, if there will be anyone who will somehow get to read this, I hope they will be like you, Mother... I admired your way of thinking, your mind, your philosophy, the way you talked so passionately about the stars, the moon, music, art, dreams, life so on and so forth. I can't help but see myself through you. I also didn't know how to deal with people. I still don't, but they don't know this, maybe some notice... all I can do is hope you're in peace, it's just hope... Mother, oh mother. Why did you have to leave?

~

If there's a way to cope with your grief, wish you could let me know. I don't want you back, somehow, I've gotten used to you not being. Now I don't have the audacity to imagine you here. My hands don't seek for yours; they are used to getting cold all night and then warmed by the sun, not by your hand's firm grip. Now they rest over the bed, as I feel your ghost they're clinched, not to hold yours but, to not hold yours. Let me know a way to forget and a better way to remember you. The one that got away but, you're no phoney love story, you were the purest, you were supposed to be there till the end of my chapters, for you were my beginning. Mother I'm only twenty and, you killed me as you left...

~

The thought of seeing you bring me to tears. You're sitting across from me, looking up with a light in your eyes. And it's so warm, this stare, my empty soul lights up and only then I see it's not empty. In this moment, you're smiling too, you're smiling at everything that has happened. Your smile assures me you are not going that easily. But then why? I am searching for you with no traces of your existence, to forget there ever was you, me, us.

~

Can you believe it? The tickers move along without you. The sun rose, it will again tomorrow, it does every morning. The moon changes like always, fluctuating. Flowers bloomed, they died, I inhaled, and I let go, I listened, I dreamt, I spoke but I won't lie, it's not the way it used to be, at least not for me...it plays in my head, every word we've ever spoken, and I smile remembering each for the millionth time to pay for the endless nights I cry myself to sleep. Oh mother, oh mother, my mother! Once it was you, but now it's me crying for you. How could you? Weren't you, my mother? Was I not young? I can't remember our last hug. Nothing, I want nothing and nobody. Not prayers, nor patients. Mother, I want you. Come back somehow or call me back to you. I'm melting in your want.

~

Am I still in prison? No. But I'm in hostage, not aunt Marjan's home. I'm praying to God, to heal me cause I'm so near, so near... That ceiling fan, that thick scarf is tempting. In this hollow room, her voices echo, her ghost laughs, I can hear them, no one talks. I think they listen to her sheer giggles too. I hear her footsteps at midnight, thumping and her bracelets, briskly clicking, sounds from heavens. Mother, will it ever get better?

~

It reminds me of her, everything reminds me of her. That day escalated quickly, I smiled back again the next day, I acted normal again, listened to music again, I danced, I laughed, I woke up every day without thinking about her again, but I did and do all of these differently since that day again. What am I becoming? Maybe if I don't look at your picture as your holding me in your floral dress, I won't think of you, maybe it's the song, it's probably the playlist, perhaps your name? Maybe if I stopped breathing, I won't think of you.

~

I'm leaving Afghanistan. Going to Iran. Tomorrow is my

flight, by this time the next morning I'll be there somewhere... but first I'll go home for the first time, after my mother's... Haven't seen my father, will say my goodbyes, after all, he's a Father to me and I don't want him to feel guilty because I took the blame.

~

Pages and pages of nothing but nothingness. Masih closed the book, and as soon as he did, the door opened. Both, Arvin and the guy rushed inside, freezing to death.

"Pour some tea, Masih!" Arvin cried, discarding his black scarf.

Masih, who was glad he could put the book back inside in time, fetched both black tea.

"What happened?" Masih strived to sound curious.

"The car is hidden and unrecognisable; tomorrow we'll make the deal." He took a sip of scalding tea.

"Isn't that a bit too much information for a kid?" The guy frowned at Arvin.

"Oh, believe me, he's not just a kid."

Chapter 31

Personal strangers

Mother, why raised me to be another victim
Lost in the streets?
Mother, your love was enough for me to believe
This world was filled with kindness and good deeds
But nothing seems to make sense
Since I learned to walk on my feet
Mother, another day bleeds
Into facing the realities

Mother, don't you watch me cry, laugh
That's natures favourite melodies
Mother, the blankets don't keep me warm.
I'm frozen inside with a heart, harder than steel
Mother, sweets don't excite me anymore
My mouth has lost its taste
But I can listen all day long
To the sweet stories that you say
Mother, another day bleeds
Into roaming around lost in streets

Mother, now the monsters live in my mind
They are no longer under my bed
They whisper all the time to pity myself
Mother, I'm not your precious little child
I've grown up, what a terrible desire

I had for years
Mother, another day bleeds
Into searching for places to find your arm's peace

Mother, why raised me to be another victim
Lost in the streets?
Mother, your love was enough for me to believe
This world was filled with kindness and good deeds
But nothing seems to make sense
Since I learned to walk on my feet

Mother, another day bleeds
Into facing the realities

Mother, another day bleeds
Into roaming around lost in the streets

Mother, another day bleeds
Into searching for places to find your arm's peace

The song ended as they stepped out of the taxi. Both cried silently through their sensitive ride, looking outside the window. Each delicately fragile, pretending to be strong. After a twenty-minute pause, Arvin broke the silence. "It's the last day. Tomorrow we'll be waiting in the operation room by now..." Arvin smiled, looking at Masih.

"And then we'll live happily ever after..."

"I don't know about that."

"What do you mean?" Masih asked.

"I think when you get life, you'll fear happy endings. There's always something left until there isn't."

"You're too pessimistic for me. Anyway, this is the last deal, right?" Masih took the last bits of his sweet bread.

"Yep." Arvin kicked the air, walking on the empty road. It was the first time Masih saw him behaving like this, so he didn't stop there and took the opportunity.

"You never told me about your family, your mother..." Masih lowered his voice.

"They're dead," Arvin said tonelessly and ended it right there as if he talked about a bunch of dead mice eventually trapped in the mousetrap.

"But you can talk to them, like the way you do."

"What?" Arvin shrieked.

"You know, the way those we love never really leave us, and we can talk to them. You said it yourself."

"Yeah, but I'm good with one," Arvin muttered.

"Who?"

And the question was born only to be left like that.

The rest of the journey, somewhere in *Sharh-e now* was silent until the cry of a baby made them turn to their left and right. Arvin stood still, watching that black Jeep as a man with grey hair stepped out, his head held high. He muttered something to the young lady, carrying the baby. She turned. The eye contact with Arvin was painful to watch.

The man glanced and ushered the women inside, and slammed the gate shut after another furious gaze at Arvin. It was hard to tell what was happening. Nonetheless, Masih could tell Arvin was battered.

Arvin gulped, and his shimmering eyes went back to dry pretty quick. He cleared his throat and let go of his tightened fists.

"Guess you robbed them bad sometime?"

Masih expected a laugh, but Arvin's pale face and expressions made him regret what he said. "Did you know them?" Masih asked.

"He's my father."

"What? But just half an hour ago, you said they died?"

"I say that to myself too."

"Why...?"

"Let's go, Masih, let's just go."

"No, I want to know!" Masih raised his voice. "How can I trust you if you don't tell me the truth?" Masih added.

"I saw you reading it, so stop acting, kiddo."

Masih drowned in shame, couldn't help but wrap his hands around his blushing face. This kept his mouth shut for the rest of the day.

~

They made a deal, and the four manly men, with their hardened expressions, thick beards, and moustaches got up from the table and left the restaurant.

Arvin let go a sigh of relief since he had been in a friendly argument, getting heated now and then, for the past three hours. He desperately endeavoured to convince them to let him have an extra five thousand to make it up to thirty, and they accepted eventually while dinner was delivered to them, smoky, fresh kebabs.

"We had an accident on our way to my wedding day. The man you saw was the one driving. A young girl died, but before he spoke a word, I took the blame. After I was bailed out, I left to see him three hours before my flight. I saw him and heard Sara's voice as she shouted out his name. He couldn't look me in the eye but said she was now our *namoos* (honour), and he had no other choice... They say it's a dishonour when once the relations had been set up. What sickening relationships, what an awful dignity we are protecting, what an outdated legacy we are carrying on. They say it's a stigma to break the bonds once it has been mend, but I'd rather own the stigma than to swallow this disgrace every second of my life..." Arvin paused. "You probably don't even know what I'm talking about..." he added, then sighed.

"No, I know... when my mother was beaten to her death. We went to her father. She went with a hope I could sense but could already predict its setback... he advised her to marry the man she was almost killed by, for she is their *namoos*. I overheard them. I don't understand us sometimes, the way we people are..." said Masih.

Arvin gulped, averting his eyes to the descending light, altering to violet dusk.

"Why didn't you do something now?"

"I feel nothing, no hate..." Arvin looked at him.

"So now what? You're just going to let them be?"

"Eventually, Masih, you just gotta befriend your past. There's nothing else you can do about it."

Chapter 32

Almost

They were back in the same house in the narrow streets of *Khair khana*. The man missing two of his front teeth was waiting for them drinking thick, black tea.

Masih kept listening to the glitching radio. Arvin hummed along to Ahmed Zahir's *"Ba Khuda tang ast delam"* while watching the candle burn, for the power cut off, again.

"Then what happened?" Masih abruptly broke the silence as they headed towards *Jamhuriat* Hospital.

"You mean how I became this, a *podari*? (addict)"

"That's not what I meant!" Masih defended himself. But It was exactly what he wanted to know.

"No, that's exactly what you meant, just say it, Masih. I suffered a lot by not saying what killed me, eventually."

"And your question is, how a boy, grown up with an alcoholic father, imprisoned for six months, lost his mother, then saw his almost-to-be wife as his stepmother, can become an addict, right? All they ask is why we're doing it; no one asks why we did it in the first place."

"So, according to you, I also should be under the bridges? Should I count my misfortunes?" Masih asked.

"Don't you dare even think about it? I'll kill you!"

"Why not?" Masih stopped. "Give me some." Masih reached for Arvin's pocket, which constantly made a crumpling sound when he would deal with something inside it at night.

"No! Don't! It's like tasting death every second, every

minute, every moment of your life!"

"Then why are you doing it?"

"There was an emptiness I thought it could fill it, but I ended up in a cavern, alone. There's a void within me I can't fulfil... and there's no use in finding a missing piece when nothing's missing. Some things exist that way, incomplete, no matter how much you want to complete, it winds up breaking you, you'll merely end up fixing yourself, so let me be..."

"Why aren't you leaving this cavern, Arvin?"

"I can't..."

"You can't what?"

"I can, I can, but the truth is, I don't want to."

"But why?" asked Masih.

"Why not?" retorted Arvin. "Masih, there's nothing for me left to look forward to when you think and think but can't find a will to live...it's a heavy feeling on my chest. I can't get rid of."

"But your mother...?" Masih muttered.

"Could you read it?"

"Yes."

"Then you know she's..."

"Weren't you the one who said that the ones we love never leave us? I don't think mothers ever die, Arvin, nor do they ever leave us, whether we like it or not. I can feel her presence every second."

"In that case, she's disgusted by me."

"For helping a son save his mother? You're giving me the world while being homeless yourself. "

"Your helplessness kills me, and my incapability is my nightmare. There's nothing more into it," Arvin snapped.

"Whatever it is, you're saving my mother, Arvin."

The silence lasted for more than Masih anticipated.

"You know? If we could save your mother, then I promise you, Masih. I'm going to quit all of what is killing me slowly."

"Then you better start from now."

199

And dear Arvins, when you're hunting for familiarity, I hope you don't get chased by what killed you before.

"So I found the missing piece?" Masih asked.

"You know what, kid? I think you were the missing piece." Arvin smiled, looking at him. "I took the flight that day but dropped out of college and found a job in a packaging factory through the guy who would be hospitalised occasionally, for being overdosed. He was offered opium when he was seventeen by the manager of the factory to make him work faster, and the same thing happened with me. Started from a cigarette, I was offered for my headache and endless complaints, and by lighting that up, I lit my life on fire. I saw him dying the day I was being deported. If there's one thing, I want you to remember of me, Masih, it's don't ever do what I did."

Suddenly, a grim whistle and a thumping sound followed it as Arvin fell on his face. First, the bag snatched, then his hair was forcefully being pulled out of his head, his blood began dripping on the cold cement. His fingers were pointed towards Masih, gesturing as each trembled, for him to go away.

Masih ran for his life. One of the four masked men followed him.

~

Amidst dust and blood and heavy punches, it was numb looking at the blue-sky spinning. Like the day he sat inside those enormous, pretty teacups with his mother, looking up, giggling. She was always around, and here she was one last time.

Her scent engulfed him lying there, her favourite rose perfume merged with the mint gum she used to chew. She stood there, smiling from the niche, ready to take his hand. Arvin, too, smiled back, waiting for it to be over.

~

Street after street, jumping over walls and crashing with the bustling crowd, Masih found himself in the same bazaar he separated from his mother after the explosion.

For a second, he wished the guy would still be following him, and he wished he carried a gun with him, so it wouldn't hurt much but still do the job. Strange ideas were coming up, jumping in front of an expensive car, and making the victim pay for his mother instead of him if he happened to make it alive. To kidnap that little girl whose mother was busy bargaining, or to steal something from everyone who came along his way.

His heart jerked, and his legs trembled. He sat on the footpath, gasping for air. Every breath he took was rooted with a mix of aversion and guilt. The sunlight filled the ground, but he kept searching for his sunken, dark eyes to see something.

A man selling mangoes continued screaming at the top of his lungs, and the next thing he heard while opening his eyes was Marzia yelling, "He woke up! He opened his eyes!" She sprinkled water on his face and helped him drink the rest.

She quickly opened his mouth and stuffed it with fruits. Marzia drew her finger over the deep scar near his eye. "Look at yourself, boy! Where have you been!"

Locks of her frizzy hair peeked out from her red scarf as she mumbled prayers while shaking her head.

She left to the kitchen to fetch more for him to eat, and Masih gained the energy to stand on his feet. He decided something while chewing those tasteless pineapples.

Masih ran to their house in search of that man's card. He still remembered a blurred vision of that house. Gul in his burgundy skin-tight, but not the guy with his bag who saved his life by his odd appearance, he didn't want to think about him, not now, not ever.

Masih raised the edge of the flower printed rug and took the dusty card which had that man in a black suit's phone number, and that was it, no name, no address, nothing. This was the decision, his doomed path.

He inhaled, picturing himself in an oversized red dress adorned with dangles, dancing himself to his death.

When he wanted to turn and leave for the telephone booth at the supermarket, Marzia screamed at the top of her lungs. The birds flew away from the window. His ears started ringing.

Marzia pushed the door open, wearing an eerie smile. He breathed for air as she threw her hands over his shoulders. "Boy, where have you been? Let's go!" she beamed.

"Where?" Masih choked.

"To your mother, come on, we don't have time."

"She's going to die, isn't she?"

"What? No! It's her operation day today. Mujeeb *jan* had given your mother's name to the red cross funding, and the required amount of money has been given by a generous man called Ayaar, probably his *zakat* for Ramadan."

Masih felt his lips curve into a smile, and tears were streamed down his parched face.

"Why would you say she is going to die?"

"That's what you said. I heard you talking to *kaka* Mujeeb."

"Oh, Masih, it's a herniated disk. Yes, it is dangerous. The doctor did say that if we don't get to do her operation in the next ten days, she will get paralysed, but look, that's not happening. Let's go now. Hurry up."

Masih wore his torn slippers. Marzia put on her boots, and off they went into a taxi on their way to the hospital.

Marzia wrapped her black scarf around her face because of the pungent smell of diesel coming from the back of the car.

It felt foreign to Masih to be happy, an outsider trying to fit in unrequited places. Marzia pointed at a spot in the street saying, "Right there, when I found you and was coming back, right there a *podari* was beaten to death. They said he was young, but I don't mind at all. I hope we get rid of them all for good."

Her curses and accusations continued, but Masih couldn't hear her anymore, staring at the abyss from the window. He reconciled with familiarity, sheer sadness, swallowing lumps of sorrows—another forsaking.

You felt so personal while being a stranger...

A grief severer than his own father.

"The operation has started ten minutes ago," said the young nurse, guiding them into the waiting room.

Marzia whispered something to the nurse.

"Well, it's an operation, ma'am, and they have consequences. We can't guarantee anything. Please just wait and pray," the nurse replied loud enough for Masih to hear.

The nurse left like his father had, but she'd be back, and he won't.

Masih crouched silently, tears streaming down his charred skin. What had a child his age done to deserve this? Was it his grandmother? Was it the Taliban? Was it poverty? Was it because of the civil war forty years back that caused all this, a never-ending trauma? Was it the Soviets? Was it God who doesn't talk to kids like him anymore? Or was it all because he had committed a terrible crime and was born in Afghanistan?

The more questions he asked, the more frantic he became. A wingless bird inside a roofless cage, hopelessly staring at the crack of light peeping into the darkness, coming from underneath the door of the room in which his mother was being cut open.

Chapter 33

Things left undone

"Brother *jan*, you better do something about her, or else she will be forced to marry a, you know...?" said Wajiba sitting next to Fardin, and she took a sip of her black steaming tea.

Fardin remained silent, but she continued after scratching her immense, black mole near her upper lip.

"They come in and check every house. They'll get sceptical after finding not one but two young girls whose family hasn't put a white flag over their house... I'm afraid for my own daughter brother *jan*. She is engaged, but they don't care, they'll force her to marry one of them if they saw, plus she's undoubtedly prettier. She's your niece, do it for her."

Fardin was someone who was not Fardin at all, only the name was the same about him, nothing else. His long beard had turned grey, his forehead deeply wrinkled. "But I don't know anyone in *Mazar-e Sharif*..." he said, looking hopelessly at his sister.

"Oh, leave that up to me." she smirked.

Rukhsaar gasped, her hands clasped across her chapped lips. She stepped back from the door and ran to the kitchen, bursting into tears. She laid her head on the polished kitchen table.

"What's wrong?" her cousin asked as she left the dirty dishes and ran to Rukhsaar.

After choking on to leaden words, she finally spoke. "Reema, my father is giving me away..."

"Well, you should be happy. That's a good thing." she beamed.

"No, I don't want to!" Rukhsaar howled.

"Shush! Be quiet. They'll hear you," Reema said, pointing at the kitchen window wrapped with plastic and covered with yellow drapes.

"Let them, I'd rather die by their filthy hands than to live a life like this!" she sobbed.

"Rukhsaar, we have no other choice. Think about your three disabled siblings. You know well about their unfortunate condition; they need special care. And your father? He's getting old. He won't be able to take care of you or protect you from these occasions. Rukhsaar, I understand how your life has turned out to be something you never even thought of. It happened to all of us. Look at me, my fiancé, the love of my life, died, and now I'm getting married to a man thirty years older than me. We have no other choice. It's how it is now."

"Why? Why must we be entitled, or rather chained to the last name of a man, to be seen with respect, otherwise we're only a threat, a thing left undone?"

"I wish I had an answer."

Reema left to her mother, calling her. Rukhsaar rubbed her red eyes and sat quietly on the chair, just like she sat when they first came for her hand. A room somewhere in Kabul bestowed to his father in exchange. And just like she sat when her mother-in-law complained about Rukhsaar's poor posture and grim face, her thin lips, and bony cheeks the first time they saw her. She sat like this when they put henna on her clammy, trembling hands. And she still sat unmoved as if she had beheld and memorized her remaining life, just like a movie.

Epilogue

The hero dies

"It all comes to an end, boy, after everything you've been through. Say my hi to your mother there," said the masked man, pointing his gun at a young boy who stared at him with his green, teary eyes.

"Mother, here I come..." he said, closing his eyes.

He stepped backwards and the short metal fence of the terrace stopped him.

The masked man pulled the trigger, and the young boy fell over the fence in slow motion.

"Cut!" Screamed the man sitting on a chair beside the rolling cameras. He gave them a standing ovation as everyone applauded them.

The young boy jumped off the stage and with the help of the crew members. He ran back upstairs and saw the director's arms wide open in ecstasy. They hugged firmly, which lasted for minutes, both sobbing.

"I'm proud of you, Masih. You did a great job. Congratulations Wish she were here to see what her son has become," he said, fighting the tears.

"It's okay, Uncle Roberson," Masih said, wiping his tears. "Whatever God wills, happens. We can't fight destiny."

The director nodded and sighed.

"Tell Miss Sara to please come out from the dressing room. It's her last shot! For the love of God!" the director howled.

Masih smiled, shaking his head. His phone lit up as it

chimed. He gulped and picked it up. "I miss you, mother."

"Masih! Masih *bachem* how did it go??"

"How else would things go when I have your prayers following me? It went great."

"Oh, *shukor!* (thank goodness) Your *khala* Marzia is here too, and so is Sherin."

"Pass my salaam to them. I'm finally coming back home Mother; I'm coming back to you."

Acknowledgements

I would love to thank the kind editors, designers and every single person involved in making this possible. Thank you for all your efforts and for believing in my story. I'll forever be in your debt. You've been the best I could ask for. I want to thank Mrs Leila Kirkconnell a qualified author who was the first reader of my book when it was just another unsolicited manuscript. She selflessly gave her time and effort to someone she didn't even know and all she asked was to pass kindness. She gave me such great advice and taught me so much.

I want to thank my talented friend Mohammad Chakhansuri for his remarkable, considerable and selfless work on the cover. The scene in the cover is a personal matter and so close to my heart, and yet I couldn't have ever brought it to life the way he did so beautifully.

I want to thank my friend Tanya Verma who made me believe in what I wrote. She said to me the words that I needed to hear the most in that specific phase of my life. It's because of her that I believe nothing is impossible, that dreams do come true.

It's not common to come across people like Mrs Leila, Mohammad, Tanya and all the kind people I've been lucky enough to get to know but sadly can't mention since it'll take pages to describe their kindness. Life's tough and words can't explain how beautiful it is when someone comes to the end of that dark tunnel with a lantern that will last forever. I'll always remind myself and get inspired by them. What they did is unforgettable.

About the Author

Samman Akbarzada is a novelist and award-winning poetess from Afghanistan. She was born in Pakistan and has spent the first nine years of her life there studying and making a memorable childhood. She's been passionate about writing since a young age. It was an on and off progress, eventually, she got more into it when she was twelve. Forthwith, it evolved as an essential part of her life.

Printed in Great Britain
by Amazon

15703577R00122